When Drazyl the sea dragon finished his story, he let out a sigh that pierced Ethan's heart.

"You must be lonely," Ethan sympathized.

"Yes," Drazyl agreed, sadly. "A dragon without people to guard is a waste of a very long life. Or was a waste." He brightened, then beamed at the boys with something close to affection. "For now I have found you two. And we can all live here under the sea, happily ever after."

Nicholas gulped. "Uh — not exactly. You see we don't *live* here. We live in Boston, and were just visiting Cape Breton for Thanksgiving."

"But you do live here," Drazyl said in a slow, sweet voice. He paused for a moment, then gave a significant thump of his spiked tail and added, "You live here *now*."

DRAGONFIRE

#2
Castle Beneath The Sea
Morgana Rhys

PRICE STERN SLOAN
Los Angeles

To Esmee

Produced by Cloverdale Press, Inc.
96 Morton Street
New York, New York 10014

Published by Price Stern Sloan, Inc.
360 North La Cienega Boulevard
Los Angeles, California 90048

ISBN: 0-8431-2716-3

10 9 8 7 6 5 4 3 2 1

One

Breaking the Rules

At ten o'clock on the morning after Thanksgiving, Nicholas Lord downed the last bit of the turkey sandwich his stepmother had packed for lunch, then scrambled out of the house to check the tide. He marched to the edge of the cliff that towered out of the sea and shielded his eyes from the slanty but bright November sun. To Nicholas's right lay the village of Frenchman's Bay. To his left the bay itself curved in a long blue arc, ending at Smugglers' Notch and the tall white lighthouse at its point.

At that very moment his father, stepmother, and about half a dozen other relatives of the recently combined Lord and Evans families were prowling the quaint, hilly streets of Frenchman's Bay, waiting for the local whaling museum to open. Nicholas and his stepbrother Ethan had begged off from the excursion, glad for the chance to escape the

1

commotion of their families' holiday celebration. It was the boys' first trip back to Cape Breton since October when Nicholas's father had married Ethan's mother and brought them along to the Lords' Nova Scotia vacation home for a chance-for-everyone-to-get-acquainted honeymoon.

"It makes it all seem so real, being back here again," Nicholas said to his nine-year-old stepbrother.

Ethan looked up from his sandwich and followed Nicholas's gaze toward the lighthouse. He lifted up his black-rimmed glasses to get a better look. The windows beneath the black roof of the lighthouse glinted in the sun, and a deliciously creepy shiver shot up Ethan's spine. Just where the shore hooked around toward Lords' Inlet, a dark spot in the distant rocks marked the very cave where he and Nicholas had stumbled into a curious adventure during their last visit. Back home in Boston, memories of his encounters with the evil sorcerer Breton and the golden dragon named Angarth in the kingdom of Nirhad had almost begun to fade away.

Almost, but not quite. Whenever Ethan fell asleep he'd have strange dreams: He'd be back in Nir again, riding dragonback on mighty, golden-scaled Angarth. Then he'd wake up and creep to his closet and pull out his old cigar box filled with special stuff. Inside were the best pieces of his miniature dinosaur collection; the autograph of his favorite author on a napkin his mother had brought back from a writers' convention; an enormous seed-cone that he was saving to plant someday, which he'd found in the redwoods while visiting his dad in California last summer; a tiny envelope with one curl of black fur from his old dog Spock who had died when he was five; and (most special of all) a small heap of shimmery purple scales that had belonged to Fingal, the young dragon he and Nicholas had met in the cave across the way, not six weeks ago.

"I wonder if the door to the Kingdom of Nir is still there?" Ethan mused aloud, staring toward the cave entrance.

"There's only one way to find out if we were only dreaming," Nicholas declared. "We can borrow Arnie Ducheyne's boat. The tide's still right. In ten minutes we can be at the cave." Nicholas's deep blue eyes sparkled at the prospect. "We can explore, say ten minutes more. Then before the tide even turns we can be back. No one would even know we'd been there."

Ethan shook his head. "No. Besides, I thought you had decided absolutely and positively that Nir didn't exist. You're the one

3

who said not to mention it again."

Nicholas kicked at the dirt. "Yeah, well, in Boston it didn't exist. The whole idea of dragons and wyrms and saving the kingdom seemed pretty dumb. But here," His voice trailed off and though there was no wind, Nicholas shuddered. "Things seem different here. Besides, it's fun to *pretend*, isn't it?"

"Nir wasn't pretend," Ethan started to argue.

But Nicholas wasn't listening. Nicholas was looking down at the shore below at Arnie Ducheyne's Fish and Tackle which was boarded up until next spring. "It's about time to head down now. We don't want to miss the tide."

"I'm not going to do it, Nicholas," Ethan said. "I'm not going to borrow Arnie's boat. Dad said we can't go back to that cave. That's that." Ethan rewrapped the remains of his sandwich, then carefully tucked the plastic bag into the pocket of his down vest. "Not that I don't want to," he added. Actually, he was afraid to head off in Arnie Ducheyne's flat-bottomed dinghy across the broad bay with Nicholas. One of Ethan's best-kept secrets—at least from Nicholas—was the fact that he couldn't swim.

"Don't be such a wimp!" Nicholas scolded, flicking his straight dark hair out of his face.

"Besides, I could go for a soda from the machine down there. No harm in *looking* at the boat, is there?"

Ethan took a deep breath. A little voice inside his head told him that borrowing Arnie Ducheyne's dinghy without permission was wrong—and going out in a boat with Nicholas was doubly wrong.

"Well?" Nicholas said impatiently. "I'm going. If you want to stay here, I'll be back in twenty minutes—or so." Without another word, he stomped down the pebbly grade toward the water and climbed into the small boat. For a moment there was only the sound of water slapping against the dinghy and the distant whoosh of a truck on the road above.

"Wait for me!" Ethan shouted after his brother. Halfway down to the boat, he stopped. "Are there lifejackets on board?"

Nicholas looked under the three plank seats. "No."

"Well let's get some at least."

"I remember seeing them during the summer," Nicholas said. "Arnie keeps them in the shed."

Ethan wheeled around and started back to the boarded-up white shed that stood to the right of the picnic tables. As he neared the shed his heart sank. There was a thick chain and padlock on the white door. "The life

5

jackets are locked up," he cried in dismay.

"We don't need them. It's not far and I'll keep the boat close to shore," Nicholas promised. He was already in the boat, and loosening the rope that tethered the dinghy to the dock.

Ethan took a deep breath and squared his shoulders. Then he marched back down to the shore and climbed into the boat, trying desperately not to rock it.

The outboard motor sputtered to life, and the boat jerked out past the dock. "You—you sure you know what you're doing?" Ethan squawked.

"Trust me," Nicholas said. He steadied the rudder, and the little dinghy settled down to a moderately bumpy ride across the calm blue waters.

Ethan squeezed his eyes shut for the first two minutes of their journey. But soon the rhythmic chug of the boat's motor, and the gentle passage over the low swell of the waves gave him courage to open first his right eye, then his left. His glasses were quickly misting up with sea spray, but still he turned his gaze shoreward, trying to scan the rocky coast. Within moments, the gabled black roof of the sprawling stone and wood house high on the hill above Lords' Inlet came into view. "Look! There's our house!"

"Careful. Don't rock the boat!" Nicholas warned sharply. For the first time, he took his eyes off the water and gave Ethan a hard look. "Haven't you ever been in a boat before?"

"Sure," Ethan said, whipping his head around. The boat rocked again with his sudden movement, and his stomach lurched along with the dinghy. "Last time we were here—when Arnie and Dad came to the cave to rescue us."

"Oh boy," Nicholas muttered softly and wondered not for the first time since his dad had married Ethan's mom, why he had to be stuck with a nerd for a stepbrother. He cut the motor slightly as he angled in closer to shore. Now the dramatic arched opening of the cave was in clear view. "Well, just don't rock the boat," he ordered.

"I'm not rocking the boat," Ethan countered, staring down into the bay. "Wow, there are fish down there!" he exclaimed, and leaned out a little farther to take a better look. Fronds of seaweed rocked beneath the surface of the water and shards of light darted between the billowy leaves.

Nicholas steered the dinghy out farther from the shore. Back at Arnie's dock, piloting the small boat right up to the cave entrance at high tide had seemed like it would be a cinch. But as he neared the rocky shore the water grew rougher. Now that he was a few yards from Lords' Inlet he realized that approaching the cave by water was going to be tricky.

Ethan's eyes were fixed on the water. Then, all at once, Ethan saw something incredible. There, beneath the shadow cast by the boat, ragged underwater boulders gave way to smooth-faced stones. He leaned over farther to get a closer look. "Hey, Nicholas, look at this!" he cried, amazed, and Nicholas whirled around in time to see his brother dangling perilously over the side of the dinghy.

"Toadbrain," Nicholas shouted. "Watch out, you're going to fall in!"

Ethan ignored him. "There's a wall down there, and pillars and turrets. There's a castle beneath the sea!" He turned to grin at his brother. Then everything seemed to happen at once. His sudden movement threw the light boat off balance just as a strong gust of wind whipped around a corner of the bay. The water surged in a high wave, then crashed down over the dinghy, washing Ethan overboard.

"ETHAN!" Nicholas shouted, grabbing the tiller to steady himself.

A second later, Ethan's blond head bobbed above the suddenly choppy water. "I can't swim!" The words sputtered from his lips, but Nicholas never heard them. Ethan went

under for the second time.

Nicholas stood up in the boat, horrified, for one long second. "I'm coming!" he shouted. Then he dived into the cold water after his brother.

Two

The Castle Deep

Nicholas surfaced from his dive, sputtering. He wiped the water from his eyes and frantically scanned the waves. Overhead and back toward the shore the sun still shone brightly, but a bank of low dark clouds was moving in from the east. "Ethan!" Nicholas shouted into the rising wind. Ethan's blond head was nowhere in sight.

Nicholas fought back a wave of panic, then gulped down a chestful of air and dived again. Though the salt water stung his eyes, he forced them open. Several yards below him and off toward the right he spotted his brother. Impossible as it seemed, Ethan was purposefully kicking his way *down* — not up — from the surface of the water.

"Ethan!" he yelled a second time and kicked his feet hard to force himself down toward the rapidly sinking figure. "Ethan!" he cried again, his voice echoing in his ears.

At that moment Nicholas realized he had opened his mouth underwater and nothing bad had happened. He hadn't choked or started to drown, and though he was still several yards beneath the surface of the sea, he could breathe. "Hey, what's going on here?" He stopped flailing at the water and began to enjoy the sensation of floating like a fish and breathing as naturally as he did on land.

"It's okay," Ethan paddled happily back up to Nicholas's side. "I can breathe here. I can talk." Then he grinned, "I can even swim."

"And the water's warm," Nicholas realized. "That's not normal for this time of year."

"Look down there," Ethan pointed past a school of rainbow-striped fish. "There are ruins."

Nicholas tried to focus on the shadowy spirelike shapes rising from the distant depths. "A castle beneath the sea? It's impossible."

"But true. I think we might have found a way back to Nir, after all," Ethan said with great delight.

A school of long-whiskered fish swooshed into view, each one as large as a kite. Ethan ducked. "Look at the size of that octopus," he exclaimed as an enormous tentacled creature pulsed by. Ethan held his breath, but the sea beast barely seemed to notice them.

They soon touched bottom. The sand was squishy beneath their feet, but walking was fairly easy. Cautiously, they skirted the entrance to another sea cave. This one glowed an eerie green, and a steady stream of bubbles betrayed the presence of something lurking just inside. Beyond the cave lay the barnacled ruins of a once-enormous wall. Fronds of seaweed billowed out of stone crevices like flags in the wind.

"Wow, it really is a castle," Nicholas exclaimed with delight, as he paddled through an arch-shaped hole in the wall. Sand from the sea floor had sifted high against the stones and it was hard to tell whether the archway had once been a door or a window. Inside, broken stairs spiraled up from shattered stone floors, ending a fathom or so below the surface of the water.

Ethan floated over the round keep, then steered himself downward to join his brother in the center of what was once the castle's great hall. Huge, broken carved columns lay at his feet, and silver, blue, and violet fish darted through the remains of an enormous stone hearth. A troop of sea horses, big enough for the boys to ride, swam by. The creatures turned all at once and seemed to stare at them. Ethan gulped and pressed himself against the side of a staircase. He had the uncanny sensation that any minute the horses would start to talk. The lead horse seemed to jerk his head toward Ethan, then led the others toward a battlement in the direction from which they had just come.

"Ethan, look what I've found," Nicholas called over to him.

Ethan stared into his brother's palm. "Money?" he asked curiously, disappointed.

"Not just money, Toadbrain. *Old* money. It's some kind of coin," Nicholas explained. " I wonder if a pirate ship sank around here. This could be buried treasure. Last summer, back in Frenchman's Bay I heard Arnie Ducheyne tell some tourists about how Smugglers' Cave used to be a place where pirates and smugglers and other outlaw types hid their loot."

Ethan frowned. "But I don't think we're anywhere near Smugglers' Cave anymore. We must be somewhere magic, like Nir. Maybe we've stumbled through one of those holes between time that Griffen told us about." He looked around, wishing the friendly Loremaster were with them to explain exactly where they were and what was going on. Loremasters, as Ethan and Nicholas had learned last time they were in Nir, were keepers of the stories of the Seven Kingdoms; their songs recounted Nir's history and were passed on from generation to generation. Griffen would certainly know the history of this place.

Ethan searched the ruins for some clue that they were back in Nir. "Maybe this castle sank off the coast of Nir itself. You know, like the one close to Fingal's cave."

Nicholas shook his head. "You mean Breton's castle. This castle doesn't look anything like that. It — well — " Nicholas didn't know *how* he knew but he was quite sure he was right. "It feels older, much older than Nir."

An icy current of water rushed like a sudden draft across Nicholas's back as if someone had opened a door somewhere and let in a blast of winter wind. He looked around, his voice a low whisper. "And more dangerous."

Ethan shuddered. The water seemed to vibrate with a low hissing sound. Quickly, he checked overhead — and found that the shadowy bottom of Arnie's boat was no longer in sight. In fact, in the short time the boys had been below the surface, the waters of the bay had turned as dark as night.

"Nicholas." Ethan started toward his brother, wondering if perhaps they had explored enough and should try to get back — if not to the boat, then at least to the shore off Lords' Inlet. "I think there's a storm brewing up there. We'd better get home."

But Nicholas wasn't paying attention. He

15

was creeping on his hands and knees, following a trail of coins that led to a massive arch. "What I wouldn't give for a metal detector," he muttered to himself. "Or a good strong magnet. A guy could get rich down here." The space beyond the arched passageway was blocked by a massive boulder.

"The trail leads this way. Funny though, it isn't just coins now. I found this." He opened his palm and showed Ethan a round red stone and a gold ring carved in the shape of a dragon. "It looks like some kind of treasure."

At the word "treasure," the low hiss they had heard earlier swelled to a thunderous roar. The water began to roil, knocking the boys to their knees.

"Watch it!" Ethan yelled, almost too late. Nicholas barely had time to flatten himself to the ground before a broken column teetered on its base, then tumbled in slow motion, inches from his head. The boys lay with their heads buried in their arms as the sea floor shook; the whole world seemed to slosh and rock around them.

Again, thunder roared from the rim of the ruins.

"Who dares invade the hoard of Drazyl, the Scourge of the Seventy Seas and Forty-four Lakes?" an enormous voice bellowed.

"Hoard?" Ethan's head popped up at the

word. He peered cautiously over his arm half-expecting to see a dragon. Instead, he saw what looked like a mountain. He and Nicholas were cowering in the sands near its base.

"Speak now, thieves, or forever be condemned to silence," the voice thundered again.

To his right Ethan could just glimpse Nicholas and the fluted edge of the fallen column. The older boy's dark head was still buried under his arm, but Ethan spied Nicholas's fist as it opened. The small cache of coins and gems spun off his palm into the current.

"Four pieces of eight, a golden ringlet, and the Ruby of the Mithrin Heights have been stolen from my hoard," declared the voice.

Again the word "hoard" drew Ethan's attention. This time Nicholas looked up, too. For then it seemed that the mountain itself began to move. Ethan forced himself to look up even higher. He craned his neck and straightened his glasses on his nose. By now the water had cleared and schools of tiny fish were angling in and out of spiked growths running up the mountain's spine.

"Nicholas!" Ethan suddenly exclaimed as the mountain twitched and sent a starfish careening into the deep. "I — I think we've found another dragon, and he's as big as Angarth!" The strong movement sent Ethan sailing upward, until he was eye to eye with the monster itself.

"Angarth!" The monster sounded as amazed as Ethan felt. He reached out a curved claw and caught the boy by the back of his jacket. He held Ethan up for closer inspection, and for a moment the monster's enormous lidded eyes seemed to cross and then uncross. Ethan could see his reflection come into focus in their colorful spinning depths. "*You* know Angarth? The king of all land-dwelling dragons? How could you possibly know him?" The dragon's eyes whirled in a confusion of vivid, angry colors.

Staring into the dragon's eyes, Ethan couldn't speak. He was spellbound into silence.

"Before you answer," the dragon went on in warning, "know that Angarth is my friend."

Nicholas got up more slowly. Cautiously, he tilted his head back trying to get a better view of Ethan's captor. The silt had settled completely now, and above his head the surface of the water was sparkling again. Nicholas didn't know quite as much about dragons as Ethan did, but he knew that he and his brother were in trouble. He had been about to pocket the trinkets from this sea serpent's hoard. And stealing from a dragon — even the smallest coin — was guaranteed to provoke the beast. Nicholas did not intend to stick around and find out what happened when a dragon was provoked. On the other hand, escaping the creature who dangled his stepbrother before his steamy snout didn't seem very likely.

"Uh — " Nicholas said the first thing that came to mind. "We weren't stealing anything from your hoard. In fact, we didn't even know you had a hoard, or that there was a dragon in these ruins."

Ethan added, "Let alone one who is Angarth's *friend*."

The dragon's barnacled eyebrows drew together in a perplexed frown. He blew a stream of breath from his mouth, and the seaweed dangling from his whiskers whipped Ethan across the shins, tickling him. "There you go again. Talking about Angarth as if he still exists."

"Of course he still exists. We saw him six weeks ago. In Nir. We helped him get his pearl back."

"The Pearl of Power, Peacemaker?" he repeated, then eyed Ethan more closely. "Are you a hero?" The sea serpent's voice softened.

Ethan blushed modestly. "Well, we both are really." He pointed down below to his brother.

"They do not make heroes like they used to," lamented the beast. Then he heaved a sigh and shook Ethan loose from his talon, watching the boy floated through the flotsam and jetsam down toward the sea floor. Ethan landed with a thump at Nicholas's feet.

"I think we'll be okay — *if* we play our cards right," Ethan murmured as he stood up and brushed himself off.

Nicholas looked skeptical.

The dragon emitted what sounded like a cross between a sigh and a cough. "I sense there is a story here." His leathery hide twitched again, and a blizzard of tiny, colorful fish fell from his coppery green scales. Then the dragon settled down on all fours, carefully encircling the boys with his long snakelike tail.

"I have not heard a story for a long time." The dragon looked Ethan up and down, then turned his gaze on Nicholas. "You wouldn't by chance be apprentices of a Loremaster would you?"

"No," both boys answered in unison.

Wanting to be helpful, Ethan piped up. "Though for a few days Nicholas pretended to be the apprentice to a sorcerer named Breton."

At the sound of Breton's name the monster snarled, and Nicholas jumped. He flashed his brother a dirty look, then quickly explained. "That's part of the story, uh — sir," he said, not quite sure how to address a dragon. "How I stole the Pearl from Breton."

"*You* stole the Pearl from that evil *UMGA-RATATHA-MAGOLABAROOOOOOM*?" the dragon cursed in disbelief.

"Yes, I did," Nicholas stood a little taller. "And if you want to hear about it, I'll tell you my part of the story. Ethan can tell you his."

Three

A Deadly Game

The dragon carefully extended one very long claw from his right talon and tapped the floor. "Sit here and spin your tale, little creature. It promises to be a good one."

Ethan gathered his courage and addressed the monster, trying to remember everything he'd learned last time he was in Nir about how to make polite conversation with a dragon. Both Fingal, the first dragon the boys had met, and Angarth, the dragon king, had been proud of their names and their lineage. Ethan cleared his throat and bowed. "Before we start, oh mightiest of dragons, we must know your name. In our land it is impolite not to tell our names to strangers."

The dragon uttered a suspicious grunt.

Ethan swallowed hard and crossed his fingers in his pockets. "Uh — my name is Ethan Lord, and this is my stepbrother, Nicholas." Ethan bowed again and Nicholas did the same. Ethan went on, "And we are not small creatures, only boys. Like young dragons — sort of like — " He remembered what he had learned about dragon life spans. "An eight-hundred-year-old young dragon — like Fingal."

"Fingal?"

"He's part of our story, too," Nicholas said, beginning to grow impatient.

"So if you'll tell us your name, we can begin," Ethan added, hoping that Nicholas's edginess wasn't irritating the dragon.

"Hmmmm," the dragon pondered. "Well, in *human* speech I am Drazyl, Scourge of the Seventy Seas, the Forty-four Lakes, Watcher of Landesferne, and the Keeper of the Castle Deep." His scales rustled as he spoke, and his deep voice bristled with pride. "I am son of Carnath, son of Laveth, son of Mathe, son of Kythe . . . " He rambled down several more generations of his genealogy before finally clearing his throat. "And you are in my king-dom beneath the sea, Landesferne . . . or what is left of it." Slowly, he turned his massive head and surveyed the ruined castle. "But that story can wait until I have heard about the Pearl."

Nicholas sighed with relief, then launched into the tale of how, not more than six weeks before, he and Ethan had stumbled into a cave at Lords' Inlet. There they found a young dragon named Fingal who was guarding a pool that was really a portal between the world of Cape Breton and the Kingdom of Nir. Fingal had been waiting for a hero to happen by and decided that Ethan and Nicholas were perfect for the job. The boys were then transported to Nir, where with the help of a loremaster named Griffen, and his daughter Olwyn, they tricked the evil sorcerer Breton, seized the Pearl called Peacemaker, and returned it to the mighty king of all dragons, Angarth. Then they helped Angarth banish the evil dragons, called wyrms, from his kingdom.

Ethan wrapped up the tale for Nicholas. "So last we heard, Angarth was going to take the Loremaster with him, while he looks for the missing King of Nir."

Drazyl's enormous fishlike eyes glowed with pleasure after the tale. "Ah, you both tell a very good yarn." He rocked back and forth thoughtfully on the base of his tail. "It will be good hearing more of your stories, over time. I would love to hear the lore of your land — where did you say you were from?"

"Boston," Ethan replied. "That's a city on the East Coast of the United States. It's pretty far from here."

"Wherever here is," Nicholas muttered,

looking at his plastic superhero watch. "I think people are going to start worrying about us."

But it seemed Drazyl's hearing was very sharp. "What people?" A hungry expression crossed his leathery face. "Where are they?"

"Up there," Ethan replied, pointing to the surface.

Drazyl snorted and a plume of steam bubbled through the water. "Do not be stupid," he snapped. "No people have lived up there for centuries — exactly fourteen and one half centuries to be exact. Not since Landesferne fell into the sea. But I hasten to the end of my tale without shaping its beginning." He eyed the boys. "Perhaps you'd like to eat first?" he asked, then shot out his right talon, snared a fistfull of fish, and mashed them.

"These are a good snack for story-telling," he said, shoving the squashed raw fish under Ethan's nose.

"Um, where we're from we generally prefer to cook our fish before eating it," Ethan said weakly.

Drazyl shrugged and popped the whole mess into his own mouth and gulped it down. "I will make my story short, because I am tired of it; I have told it to myself so many years now." He sighed deeply, then began.

"One day, Urdragon, who lives coiled about

the heart of Eyrth, rose up and stretched and gave a mighty roar. Mountains that towered high tumbled into the sea." The dragon paused to pound the water, and the boys were sent tumbling head over heels in the swell. Drazyl grinned with satisfaction and continued his tale. "Then the seas rose over the shores and swallowed whole kingdoms. It was a time of great sadness for human and wizard and dragon alike. My kingdom was buried here, and my castle and my hoard. The people all were swept beyond the power of my magic and drowned before I could move to save them. Now I am all alone."

The sigh that ended Drazyl's story pierced Ethan's heart. "You must be so lonely," he said.

"Well, for a dragon of my stature, not having people to watch over is a waste of a very long life. Or *was* a waste." He brightened, and his mossy scales actually seemed to gleam. "For I have found you two. I have hoped for ages beyond counting that a human would cross my path. I have stirred the waters hoping for storms, so that ships would wreck and the survivors would find their way to me. But no ship has passed this way. It seemed there were no people left. Yet now there are two of you." Drazyl regarded the boys with something close to affection. "And we can all live happily ever after."

Nicholas gulped. "Uh — not exactly. You see, we don't *live* here. We live in Boston really, and we were just visiting Cape Breton for Thanksgiving, and then this storm came up and seems to have opened up one of these holes in time that Griffen told us about. But we can't stay here — "

"Nice as it is and all," Ethan added.

Several sets of lids slammed shut over Drazyl's eyes. Though veiled, they still glowed like huge round lamps. "But you do live here," the dragon said in a slow, sweet voice. "*Now*."

Nicholas folded his arms across his chest. "We can't live here. Our family will miss us. Our parents think of us the way you think of your whole kingdom."

"What if we made a bargain with you?" Ethan went on quickly.

"A bargain?" Nicholas and Drazyl said in unison.

Nicholas rolled his eyes. His stepbrother's bright ideas had gotten them both into trouble more than once. Especially when it came to dealing with dragons.

Ethan cleared his throat and addressed Drazyl. "You said that once there were people who lived near the shore, but I bet there were other kingdoms, farther inland from here.

Weren't there?"

Drazyl scraped his talons down the bony scales of his head, as if trying to remember something from very long ago.

"Yes, of course there were people. Many kingdoms and fiefs. I know my people had enemies to the west of Landesferne."

"So that means it's likely some people survived that time of destruction. What if we could bring you and those people together?"

"You'll bring me people?" Drazyl's several pairs of eyelids snapped up and his eyes whirled around.

"Tons of people."

Drazyl lowered his head until he was eye to eye with Ethan. "How many?" he asked, beginning to sound suspicious again.

"Can't say," Ethan replied quickly.

"But enough to look after, certainly more than *two*." Nicholas whacked Ethan on the back. Sometimes being brainy wasn't so bad after all.

"That's right, more than two," Ethan promised.

"When?" Drazyl tapped his front claw impatiently.

"Can't say that either," Ethan answered, managing to sound cockier than he felt at the moment.

"But certainly not until we get out of here,"

Nicholas added craftily.

Drazyl glared hard at the boys. Then he mumbled to himself in a language neither boy understood, except for a word or two of good old American English that seemed to be sprinkled in with the more ancient tongue. "Umgrarth bonebyth, nothing to rumbyth fryth but nothing to lose either. Umdroomboombath." At last he said, "I will play this game with you."

"Game?" Nicholas eyed the beast carefully.

"Call it what you will." Drazyl actually seemed to smile. "But there is a time limit, as in every good game. By the next full moon." He stopped and repeated himself carefully, this time stressing the word *next*. "You bring me people by the *next* full moon, and I will help you open the door to your land of Cape Breton again. You can go home then. If you do not bring people to me, you stay with me forever beneath the sea."

Forever? Nicholas swallowed hard and squeezed his eyes shut. He tried to picture the moon the night before, over Frenchman's Bay. Was it waxing or waning? He had no idea because the sky had been cloudy. Last time they were in Nir, time passed more quickly than it did back home. "Did you say the *next* full moon?" he started to ask.

But Ethan was too quick for him. "It's a

deal," he said, offering his hand to Drazyl.

The dragon stared. With a swift movement, his claw shot out and snared Ethan by the hem of his sweater. Then his claw pricked Ethan's wrist.

Ethan yanked his hand back and watched in horror as a long welt surfaced on his skin then sank again and turned into a colorful picture of a coiling sea wyrm. Before Nicholas knew what was happening, the dragon tattooed him as well.

"My sign will keep both of you true to your word," Drazyl said with satisfaction. Uncoiling his tail, he gestured for the boys to start up the steps behind him. "Go up this way and you'll find a patch of bright blue that will lead you to land. Follow the sun to the west and remember, return by the next moon."

The boys didn't wait to hear any more. They didn't want to give Drazyl a chance to change his mind. With Nicholas leading the way, they slipped up the slick-surfaced stairs and began their ascent from the castle beneath the sea.

Four

Stranded

Drazyl proved true to his word. "There's light up ahead!" Nicholas shouted, and doubled his pace up the rough-hewn steps. First his head emerged from the water, then his shoulders. A few seconds later he hoisted himself onto the narrow ledge of a grotto. Deep blue water lapped at his feet, and above his head a ring of azure sky shone where a chunk of the sea cave's roof had broken.

Ethan emerged a moment later, his blond hair plastered to his scalp but his face bright with relief. "At least we know Drazyl can be trusted," he announced. Then he looked around. The sea cave, which was shaped like a horseshoe, was really just a shallow indentation in the black cliff rising from the sea. Through the entrance to the cave Ethan could see whitecaps on a blue ocean.

There was a chill in the air that set both boys shivering. "We can't just stand here,"

Nicholas said, stomping his feet for warmth. "The sun looks warm enough to dry us off. We'd better get out of this cave before we freeze."

"You don't have to convince me," Ethan grumbled through chattering teeth.

Nicholas pressed his back against the slimy dark wall. Spreading out his arms, he cautiously edged his way around to the right side of the grotto entrance. His fingers probed the mossy wet surface of the stone, then he felt up a little higher and grinned as he touched dry warm rock. "I don't think the waves ever reach much higher than our heads." Holding on to the inside cave wall with one hand, he swung himself out over the water and looked around the corner. The grotto was perched at the very end of a narrow strand of black-pebbled beach, not so different from the beach they'd landed on in Nir. The air was salty and sweet.

Nicholas ducked back into the grotto. "We're okay. Drazyl told us there might still be a beach here, and there is. Just feel your way along the wall, like I did, then hold on tight and take one big step, and you'll be on solid ground."

"Here goes nothing," Ethan murmured. Mimicking his stepbrother, he cautiously felt his way along the wall. Once or twice he had a close call as chunks of the soft cave floor fell away from beneath his feet, but he made his way to the entrance.

"Come on!" Nicholas urged impatiently from somewhere outside.

"I'm coming," Ethan replied, then took a deep breath, closed his eyes, and swung himself over the water and back a bit. He tumbled in a heap to the very edge of the stony beach. "I did it!" he congratulated himself, then noticed Nicholas, who had already scaled the rocky cliff that housed the sea cave and was busy scanning the distance.

"So, is there a town or something?" Ethan asked, bending down to wring the water out of his jeans.

"Not a thing — anywhere. Not even a sea gull." Nicholas's voice fell with disappointment. "I knew there was some catch in all of this. You just can't trust a dragon."

Ethan's instinct told him that dragons seemed to be pretty honorable, if crafty, creatures. If a dragon struck a bargain, it might *try* to get out of it, but in the end it kept its promise. Ethan also sensed that Drazyl was lonely enough to take a chance that the boys would bring him people to protect.

"I'm sure that if Drazyl told us there were once kingdoms farther inland, he was speaking the truth," Ethan assured Nicholas.

"But when, Toadbrain? *When?*" Nicholas asked, exasperated. "These dragons have a pretty wild sense of time. I mean, Drazyl's probably been alive for thousands of years, and just think of what's happened on Earth over a few thousand years or so. Lots of people have vanished. Countries' boundaries have changed. There may not be people within *twelve* 'full moons' of here." Half to himself he added, "And we don't even know when the next full moon is!"

Ethan winced. "So what should we do?"

"Dry off. Then — " Nicholas shrugged. "I don't know what to do next. But I can't walk anywhere with wet socks and shoes. The sun's high and warm now. We'd better take advantage of it."

With a great deal of trouble, Ethan made his way up the cliff. He unlaced his sneakers and spread his socks out next to Nicholas's to dry.

For a few minutes the boys stared glumly out across the sandy landscape, considering their plight. Finally Nicholas said sarcastically, "Exactly what *are* we going to do about Drazyl?"

Ethan's reply was instant. "Find people, of course."

"Toadbrain, there *are* no people. Look." Nicholas grabbed his stepbrother by the shoulder and forced him to look past the narrow strip of beach.

Nicholas suddenly realized that they had another problem. Even if they did find people, it didn't seem fair, really, to bring them back to Drazyl to be his prisoners. Nicholas began to chew on his lower lip. "I don't know about this people business," he muttered.

"But we promised Drazyl," Ethan cautioned. "You don't promise a dragon something and then break that promise."

"Thank you for the lesson, Mr. Dragon Expert. Look, why don't we follow the sun, just like Drazyl said, but not to find people." Even as Nicholas spoke, the vague thoughts in his head began to shape themselves into a real plan of action. "No. We'll find our way back to Nir. Angarth and Griffen are probably back by now and — OWWWWWWW!"

"What's the matter?" Ethan asked.

"My — my — ar — mmmm." Nicholas could barely get out the words. He fell back on the cliff and lay writhing on the ground, his left hand clutching his right arm.

Ethan looked on in horror. "Nicholas," he gasped, "it's alive. The tattoo on your wrist — it's — it's *squirming*!"

"Get it off me, Ethan. Get it off!" Nicholas shouted.

Ethan paled at the thought of touching the

wriggling sea wyrm that was wrapping itself tightly around Nicholas's wrist. But there was no one else to help him. Ethan started to reach for Nicholas, then he remembered something. He cupped his hands and shouted into the wind. "Nicholas didn't mean it! He was thinking of going to Nir to find more people for the great scourge of the Seventy Seas and Forty-eight, or however many, Lakes."

Nicholas sat up and stared at his brother. A moment later he realized the wyrm on his wrist had loosened its grip. "That creep," he muttered. "I knew we couldn't trust him. These tattoos are brainwashing devices, like the ones aliens implant in science fiction movies."

"Whatever they are, they work," Ethan muttered. In a loud clear voice he added, "Like we will work to help make Drazyl less lonely."

Nicholas took the hint. "Right. We'll rest here, and then go look for people. I just remembered the maps I saw in Breton's study back in Nir. There's a wasteland to the east of Nir, which I think lies west of here."

To Ethan's ears that didn't sound very promising, but Nicholas's declaration that he intended to serve Drazyl seemed to do the trick. Although Nicholas's wyrm tattoo remained coiled around his wrist, it relaxed its grip. Ethan's tattoo was still stretched in a wavy line from the back of his hand up his forearm.

"So that settles that," Nicholas sounded defeated. "These cute little tattoos are Drazyl's way of making sure we do what he wants." He looked once more in despair at the sunny but bleak landscape sloping upward beyond the beach. "Except there aren't going to be any people to find and we'll be stuck here forever."

"Let's just take this quest a step at a time," Ethan suggested. "And drying ourselves out here is step one. Then we wait until midday has passed, and the sun will show us which way is west."

The two boys talked some more about Nir and their parents back home, but soon the rhythm of the waves below and the warmth of the noonday light lulled them to sleep.

The song coming off the water woke Nicholas first. The singer was too far off for him to make out the individual words, but the melody was soothing and lovely and sad all at the same time.

Ethan yawned and rolled over onto his arm. "What's that?"

"Music," Nicholas replied dreamily, then in a flash remembered where he was. He sat bolt upright and blinked. Their underwater adventure with the sea dragon hadn't been part of some scary dream. One look around the deserted beachfront and he knew he was no-where near Cape Breton. The sun was defi-nitely lower in the sky, and the way west was clear now: over the narrow rib of black sand, toward the dunes and the distant horizon. But the music came from the east, from the waters behind them. "Someone's coming," he cried.

Ethan scrambled to his knees and followed the direction of Nicholas's pointing finger. Sure enough, not far off, rocking its way through the curling breakers, was a small bark boat. A square violet sail billowed out from a thin sapling mast. But strangest of all, the boat sailed against the prevailing wind as if it moved not with the sea breeze, but with a mind of its own. At its helm stood a slight, cloaked and hooded figure, its hands strum-ming a lute. "The music's coming from the boat," Nicholas exclaimed. He was on his feet at once, waving and shouting across the water. "Hey, out there. We need help!"

Ethan cupped his hands and joined in. "HELP!!!"

The hooded figure turned its head. From where they stood the boys couldn't make out the face. For a moment the little boat hovered on top of the waves. The sail went slack as the wind died. Then the figure lifted a hand and waved to them. With that gesture the cloak slipped back, revealing the sleeve of what looked like a dress.

"It's a girl," both boys moaned in unison, but for different reasons.

"I can't send a girl down to Drazyl," Nicholas muttered.

"You weren't thinking of sending whoever came to help us down to the dragon, were you?" Ethan said, horrified.

"We promised him people, and — "

"That stinks," declared Ethan.

"I know — it was just a thought. But now that we found a girl — "

Ethan carefully started down the rock. "The girl's found us, and she's coming this way. I just hoped — when I saw that boat — it might be Griffen. He had a little boat just like that. Now, *he* could have helped us out of this mess."

Nicholas had stopped listening. He eased himself down, his fingers gripping the top of the cliff. The drop to the sand was only six feet or so. He dangled a moment, then landed softly on the pebbled ground. The boat had gotten caught in the breakers about half a mile down the beach from where he stood.

Nicholas jogged over to help the girl ease the boat onto shore. "I get the feeling," he called back to Ethan who was still at the base

39

of the cliff, "she's the one who needs our help right now." But even as he watched, the boat seemed to find its own smooth path over the rolling surf and skidded smoothly onto shore. The girl climbed out, slung her lute across her back, and started toward them. She was just a yard or so away from the boys when a gust of wind skipped off the waves and blew her hood back. A mane of golden waves tumbled down her slender shoulders all the way to her waist. Her blue eyes were dark with worry, but she smiled when she saw the boys.

Nicholas ran a hand through his hair and grinned. "It figures," he said. "It figures she'd turn up."

Five

Friend in Need

Ethan stood staring at the girl, unable to believe what he saw. "Olwyn," he said at last. "What are you doing here?"

The Loremaster's daughter didn't seem the least bit surprised to see the boys. "Ethan, Nicholas. I knew I'd find you somewhere, but," she looked around the bleak seascape and frowned, "not here."

Carefully lifting the strap over her head, Olwyn held the lute in one hand, then shook off her cape. She wore a simple dress of darkest red, and around her neck hung a familiar silver dragon's claw.

"You're wearing the Loremaster's Claw of Power," Nicholas said. "I guess that means your father still hasn't come back." When the boys had left Nir six weeks before, Griffen had set out on a journey with Angarth, the king of dragons, to find Nir's missing king. With Griffen gone, Olwyn had

41

become Loremaster of Nir.

Olwyn gazed down at the sand and bit her lip. "No," she answered. "He isn't back. I don't know where he is." When she looked up, she was blinking back tears. "I need your help. Something has happened to my father. That's why I hoped I could somehow draw you back from your world — though I expected you to turn up back in Nir." She shielded her eyes from the glaring sun and shook her head. "I don't understand how you landed in the Long Waste of Cynwyd on the shores of the Guarded Sea. You are in the Eastern Reaches of the Seven Kingdoms, leagues from Nir."

Nicholas looked at Olwyn with dismay. "*You* called us back here?"

"Don't sound so happy about it," Olwyn said sarcastically. "I didn't know you had so many other friends around here." She turned on her heel and was about to walk off when Nicholas grabbed her arm.

"Olwyn, that's not what I meant — " He ran his fingers through his hair. "We thought landing back in your time was some kind of accident."

Ethan snorted. "It *was* an accident. And all my fault too. I should never have gotten in that boat — or fallen overboard."

"Was there a storm?" Olwyn asked.

42

"No," Ethan replied. "I saw a castle beneath the sea."

"A *what* beneath the sea?" Olwyn frowned and looked out over the waves. "You know, there's an old ballad about a castle beneath the sea . . . but I never thought there was any truth to it. Still, these *are* the Eastern Reaches near Cynwyd."

Nicholas shrugged. "So don't believe us. The castle's there, no matter what you think. Or," he added with a decidedly wicked glint in his eyes, "maybe you'd like to see for yourself. There's a stairway right inside that cave." He pointed toward the black outcrop of rock and the grotto.

Olwyn stared back at him a moment, then started determinedly toward the grotto.

"Don't you dare," Ethan cried. He gave Nicholas an angry look, then bounded after the girl. "He's not kidding — there *is* a castle down there, but you don't want to go near those stairs."

Olwyn just laughed and continued toward the entrance to the underwater cave. Desperate, Ethan grabbed her sleeve and pulled hard. Olwyn, who was two years older than Ethan and about four inches taller, easily plucked the heavy fabric from his fingers. She almost turned away again, then stopped, her eyes searching his face. "You're really afraid of something, aren't you? You aren't making all this up."

"No," Ethan said. "Why would we, anyway?"

Nicholas caught up with them, and Ethan turned his back on him. "Hey, I wouldn't have really let Olwyn go down there to keep Drazyl company," Nicholas said.

Olwyn looked from Nicholas to Ethan and back to Nicholas again. "I'm not sure what it is you two are talking about, but did I hear you mention the name 'Drazyl'?" Her voice was wary.

"He's the guardian of that wrecked castle we saw," Ethan explained. "His hoard is heaped in what's left of the castle's great hall. He said it was part of the kingdom of Landesferne, which is where I suppose we are, though you called this place something else."

"Cynwyd," Olwyn murmured thoughtfully. "If you weren't from another place in time, I wouldn't believe you. The tale of Landesferne and the Saga of the Great Upeyrthing is one of the ballads loremasters teach the children of the Seven Kingdoms. I always thought it was just a fairy tale."

"Believe me," Nicholas said, "Drazyl and that castle down there are no fairy tale. If you don't believe us, look at this." He pointed to the tattoo on his wrist, and Olwyn's eyes opened wide with surprise.

"The sign of the sea wyrms," she whispered in awe. "There's great power in those markings. Any creature who can practice skin-shaping must be mighty indeed, and of a very ancient time."

She bit her lip then asked softly, "Is it alive?" Gingerly, Olwyn touched the tail of the serpent coiled around Nicholas's wrist. Before their eyes it writhed slightly, though this time it didn't tighten.

"It's alive all right," Ethan told her. "And worse than that, if we even think of not keeping the promise we made, the sea dragon — the tattoo — starts to strangle us."

Olwyn fell silent. She fingered the deep folds of her dress, then cleared her throat. "And what exactly did you promise this dragon?"

Nicholas lowered his eyes. "To find people to keep him company — forever — so that we can go home."

Olwyn gasped. "And you almost sent me — "

"No." Ethan leapt to his stepbrother's defense. "He really meant what he said before. Even before he knew who you were, he said he'd never send a girl down there."

"Oh, shut up," Nicholas said, annoyed. "The point is, Olwyn, you said you needed our help to find your father, and we can't leave here until we find Drazyl some people to take care of."

Olwyn blew out a sharp breath. "I can't believe you promised him something so awful."

"There didn't seem to be any choice," Ethan said quietly.

"I thought we could just get out of there, and then forget about our bargain." Nicholas looked ruefully at his wrist. "But we can't."

Olwyn made her way over to the high black cliff, and sat down on a small ledge near the bottom. "No, you have no choice now. You can't break a promise made to a dragon. But," she added with a note of hope in her voice, "you never know how these things turn out. Perhaps whatever people you find will *need* a dragon as much as he needs them." She seemed about to go on, then cut herself off.

"Do you know something we don't, about Cynwyd?" Nicholas asked.

"Not exactly," Olwyn said looking up at him. "But meeting up with Drazyl, and promising to bring him people was probably no accident — just like our meeting here. I feel as if I'm at the beginning of a new story in the lore of the Seven Kingdoms. An important one."

Nicholas shifted uneasily. "Whatever

story's about to happen, I don't think we should be wasting time here, and neither should you. Drazyl gave us a time limit. And you've got to find your father soon, since you sense he's in danger. How can we help you? You're the Loremaster now yourself; you probably have at least some of your father's powers."

Olwyn let out a silvery laugh. "Oh, but I'm only eleven years old. I haven't reached my full powers yet. I can command the winds a little, and work spells of healing with my music, but I can't do much more than that. To tell the truth," she went on, "I don't know how you're supposed to help me. I only know that in the last dream my father sent me there was some kind of trouble he couldn't transmit, but there was one clear instruction: Find Ethan and Nicholas again, and bring them back. They are needed."

"Where was he?" Ethan asked softly, almost afraid to hear the answer, for even as Olwyn spoke he got a distinct feeling of some place cold and high and icy with winter wind.

Olwyn shook her head. "I don't know," she whispered. "I couldn't tell, and I don't remember anything at all about the dream, except that I was to find you. My powers aren't even good enough to do that yet. I summoned you, and you turned up a month's journey from

Nir, already under oath to help one of our world's most fearsome and ancient dragons."

"So what do we do now?" Nicholas asked. "There must be something we can to do help you and find people for Drazyl at the same time."

Olwyn smiled. "There's a song about Landesferne, and what happened when it sank off the Waste of Cynwyd. According to the story, Cynwyd became very powerful after Landesferne vanished from the earth. What matters now is that I have tracked my father for over a month. The most recent rumor of his travels with Angarth brings me here — or rather to Cynwyd. The town itself is a day's walk from here."

"So let's get going," Nicholas said. "Maybe we can find your father there." He sounded hopeful. "And if we find people, maybe we can convince some of them to come back with us and at least meet Drazyl."

"Too bad we can't convince Drazyl to leave his castle beneath the sea and move close to a town," Ethan said.

"He won't leave his hoard. No dragon will," Olwyn said. "But why do I get the feeling that there are *no* dragons around here? As if there's a kind of. . ." she shivered slightly as she searched for the right word, "empty space in the world around here."

48

"Perhaps Drazyl has cast a spell of invisibility," Nicholas suggested, "so other dragons won't find him and steal from him."

Olwyn looked only half-convinced. "I've heard of such things, but there's something else. Some other power at work. I can't quite put my finger on it."

"Standing here and talking isn't getting us anywhere," Nicholas said impatiently. "Let's get going."

Olwyn agreed. "The sun will soon set, though we'll have the light of an almost full moon."

Nicholas and Ethan exchanged a nervous glance. "*Almost* full?" Ethan repeated with a gulp.

"The full moon's three days off," Olwyn said.

"Three days?" the two boys echoed.

"That's barely enough time to get to Cynwyd and back," Ethan said with a sinking heart. "Even if the people *were* willing to come with us."

Six

Circle of Fear

Nicholas helped Olwyn pull her boat safely above the tide line. Ethan sorted her provisions, dividing them into four piles: one for each to carry, one to leave safely stowed in her boat. Then they set off toward the west. "Well, if Drazyl and the kingdom of Landesferne lie beneath the sea, Cynwyd should be that way," Olwyn pointed west. A range of low weedy dunes blocked the view. Quickly, the small party clambered across them. Two more hills of dunes lay beyond, followed by low scrubby brush.

They traveled until sunset, when Olwyn decided to camp for the night. "We could wait for moonrise," Olwyn told them, "then continue through the night, but the closer we get to Cynwyd, the stronger the feeling grows."

"That there's some kind of empty space in the air?" Ethan wasn't sure he understood what Olwyn meant, but he trusted her instincts.

Olwyn nodded. "I'd rather travel by day. If we stop now, we'll reach the outskirts of the town by late afternoon tomorrow. It will be light enough to get our bearings, but dark will come soon enough to hide us — should there be the need."

Late the next afternoon, the three travelers stopped at the top of the last low hill before the broad valley of Cynwyd.

Olwyn turned slightly north and pointed beyond the spreading limbs of the one full-sized oak. Brown leaves still clung to its branches and rustled in the breeze. "Down there is the town of Cynwyd."

The boys looked over the plain. Though the exact distance was hard to judge from where they stood, the settlement seemed to be only a couple of miles away. Tightly clustered spires and roofs pierced the sky above a stout encircling wall.

"Its bigger than Nir," Ethan remarked.

"But there's no castle here," Olwyn told him. "Cynwyd has never had a king — as far I know."

Nicholas squinted to see better. "What's going on down there?" he asked. "My eyes are good, but not good enough — "

"Blessed be the Pearl!" Olwyn cried. The

delight in her voice surprised him. "We've arrived in time for the autumn fair. Cynwyd's famous for its dyed cloth and woven goods. My mother's silks, that I wear, came long ago from a Cynwyd fair!" She hurried down the slope. As soon as she stepped beyond the reach of the old oak tree's broadest branch, she staggered. "Ooooooh!" she moaned.

"Olwyn!" Ethan cried in dismay. He reached her side just as she fainted.

Nicholas pushed Ethan out of the way and knelt by the girl. "Get some water," he ordered.

Ethan looked around. The land was bone dry. Then he remembered the wooden flask of water in Olwyn's pack. His hands trembled as he untied the leather thongs. "She's alive, isn't she?" he asked as he handed the flask to his brother.

Before Nicholas could answer, or even sprinkle water over Olwyn's pale face, her eyelids fluttered. Her blue eyes opened and she looked from Nicholas to Ethan, as if she had never seen them before. She blinked a couple of times, then pressed her fingers to her temples. A moment later recognition flickered in her eyes.

Nicholas eased her up into a sitting position. "What happened?" he asked, worried.

Her face was still pale and her hands as cold as death.

"That tree." She looked back over her shoulder, and leaning on Nicholas struggled to stand up. She gulped down some of the water from the flask and the pink returned to her cheeks. "That tree marks the boundary."

"Of what?" Ethan asked, looking first to the left of the tree and then the right. No fence or wall was in sight.

"I don't know," Olwyn admitted. "Not exactly. I only know when I passed the tree I felt as if a cold hand reached into my chest and squeezed my heart." She blanched at the memory, and Ethan was afraid she might faint again, but Olwyn tossed her hair off her face and blew out her breath. "I crossed over a Circle of Power." Then she regarded Nicholas with surprise. "Didn't either of you feel it?"

They both shook their heads.

"Maybe because you're almost a full-fledged loremaster you're more sensitive than we are to magic," Nicholas suggested.

"But who made it?" Ethan asked.

"And what does it do?" Nicholas inquired.

"I have no idea." Olwyn bit her lip and a tired, worried expression crossed her thin face. "I only wish my father or Angarth were here. All I know is whoever made it has great power, and its spell must somehow be

53

connected to making Cynwyd a desert."

"Whatever spell it is, we don't *seem* to be affected by it." Nicholas studied Olwyn, then his brother. "You both look okay to me."

"I noticed that too," Olwyn considered that fact a moment, then shrugged. "We're inside the circle now, and I think we might as well continue on to Cynwyd. Let's just remember that the circle begins on this side of that tree, and it probably continues all around the circumference of the town. Remember this spot. If anything should separate us, be sure to come back here, cross over the circle if you can, and wait for the others. That rock there," she pointed to a distinctively jagged boulder, "will be our meeting place. Its shape will be visible even by the light of the moon."

They proceeded down to the plain. Snatches of music from the fair wafted toward them on the wind. As they drew near they spied bright tents and pavilions.

"There are so many people!" Ethan remarked, and started to smile. "It's like the firefighter's carnival I went to on Martha's Vineyard last summer."

"What do they sell in the booths here?" Nicholas asked Olwyn. "Are there games? I'm really great at knocking over pyramids of bottles with balls. I can win you a prize," he informed her eagerly.

"We have games too, but I have never heard of throwing balls at bottles. There are races, and the hurling of stones and climbing of posts by the strongest men of each clan. Mainly the fair is a time for tradesmen to display their wares, and for jugglers to entertain, and there is much music and feasting."

Olwyn stopped the boys at the outskirts of the fairgrounds. She pulled them over to one of the tall stone pillars wrapped with gay bunting and topped with colorful banners. "We must be careful here. This place *looks* harmless enough," she said, "but we are within a circle of enormous power. I don't know who or what holds the spell to this place — or if the spelling will even affect us — "

"It made you faint back there," Ethan said with a shudder.

Olwyn nodded. "But so far nothing has happened to change any of us. We should, first of all, stick together. And then," she looked down the fair's main concourse, then off to one of the smaller lanes of booths, "we have to disguise you somehow. Dressed the way you are, people, maybe the *wrong* people, may notice you."

"But we don't have money to buy clothes," Nicholas said, eyeing the colorfully costumed crowd.

The clothing was very similar to the style in Nir. Women were draped in long dresses,

55

some with overskirts, some with aprons, all with billowy or puffed or pleated sleeves. The men wore sleeveless tunics or jerkins over loose-sleeved shirts. Instead of pants they wore tights and boots. But the clothes were dyed brighter colors, worked more intricately with embroidery and even gold thread, and the fabrics were rich and sturdy.

"What do you do for money here?" Ethan asked.

"You mean coins?" Olwyn looked worried. "I have some, fortunately. But I don't need coinage, usually. I barter my needs for a song, or a tale or small spell when necessary. But here I would rather not use my powers — not until I know exactly where the heart of the evil lies."

She told the boys to wait between the alley of tents and headed off alone for one of the dingier outlying stalls. Quickly she selected some secondhand clothing for them as well as two large pieces of cheap printed cotton. Ten minutes later, she returned to them carrying her purchases. "Here," she said, handing Nicholas a long suede sleeveless tunic. "Now you'll look more like another journeyman trader." She told them to wrap their jackets in the squares of cotton. Carrying these bundles they would look like they were travelers who had come to the fair for fun and trading.

Nicholas slipped the vest over his sweatshirt. It was large. Nevertheless, it served to hide his worn jeans and so hide the fact that he was not wearing the customary tights or leather breeches worn by local men and boys.

Ethan wasn't quite as lucky. The one cheap shirt small enough for him was very worn and of a scratchy, poor quality wool that was rather uncomfortable. "And what am I supposed to be?" he mumbled as he tried to reach a particularly itchy spot on his upper back.

"The younger apprentice to — " Olwyn stopped to think. Then she grinned. "A wine merchant from Nir. That should open some doors for you. And I," she turned to Nicholas, "am your sister."

"Wouldn't it be easier just to say who you really are?" Ethan suggested. "And ask if anyone has seen your father?"

"No," Olwyn said. "Anyone who would cast such a spell around the town is not to be trusted, and would surely not befriend a loremaster." She checked both boys' clothing one last time. "You both will pass — besides, people at the fair don't watch each other *that* carefully. I suspect they're too busy having fun. And no matter what evil lies ahead on our quests, let's at least enjoy ourselves as much as we can here. Don't forget, if we lose each other, to head right back out of town and up the hill to the rock beyond the tree."

Seven

Side Show

The excitement of the jostling fair crowd was contagious. Ethan almost forgot their quest and the danger of the circle of power as he wandered past the colorful stalls. Fragrant meat pies and iced pastries tempted him to spend the few coins Olwyn had given him while they were disguising themselves. Meanwhile, Nicholas lingered over booths devoted to games of chance, mystified by the multicolored dice and intricately patterned gameboards painted directly on the dry earth.

Olwyn lost herself in an avenue of stalls tended by fabric merchants from the farthest reaches of Luthmyn and Rhondyr. She led the boys to what must have been the tiniest, most crowded stall in the entire fair. "These are *real* Rhondyrian silks," she murmured, fingering the bolts of brilliant scarlet, azure, and emerald material.

"Do not touch what you cannot pay for,

girl," the bearded Rhondyrian vendor snapped. Then he spotted Olwyn's lute. "Though if you have a true gift for song, then I might barter an evening of entertainment for my family and guests back at the tent."

Olwyn looked longingly at the azure silk that shimmered with a green leafy pattern. Then she set her chin. "No, I have no skill." Ethan's eyes widened, not just because Olwyn was lying, but because she had managed to disguise her voice. It sounded harsh and rough and unable to carry the simplest of tunes.

"Nor money, I am sure." The merchant turned gruff and waved the trio away from his wares.

Olwyn put the incident behind her and darted down another row of stalls, pausing to look at a display of dresses stretching over a counter.

Nicholas gave a bored sigh. He looked back at Olwyn, then shrugged. After all, if they did really lose each other in the crowd, they had already arranged a meeting place. He plunged back down the aisle of dressmaker stalls and onto the main concourse.

"Wait for me," Ethan called out. Nicholas slowed down just enough to let him catch up. They emerged at the edge of the crowd at the left of a small raised stage.

A puppet show had just begun. The marionettes were dancing from strings so fine they might have been woven from a spider's web. But it wasn't the lavish costumes or the incredible skill of the puppet master that made Ethan catch his breath. He grabbed his stepbrother's arm and gasped. "They look like they're alive!"

Nicholas nodded, unable to find his own voice. He was spellbound by the sight before him: people dressed in costumes like those he'd seen in Nir, and now Cynwyd. Miniature men, women, children, and even animals, that seemed as alive as the people watching in the crowd: eyes that blinked, smiles that seemed real, hands and arms that bent as if they were made of human flesh and blood, not paste and wire and wood; and tears — there were a surprising number of puppets weeping clear, perfect tears.

Nicholas edged his way closer to the platform. A tear glistened on the wrinkled cheek of an old woman puppet who was rocking a baby to sleep. The tear seemed so real; he had to touch it to be sure. His hand crept toward the apron of the little stage. *THWACK!* His hand hit an invisible but very solid surface and what felt like an electrical current shot through him. He cried out in pain, but a gale of laughter from the audience drowned out his

60

cry. Nicholas tapped the air gently with his finger. Sure enough, the barrier was there. But why?

Ethan danced from foot to foot nervously as he watched his brother. "Hey, remember what Olwyn said," he urged. "Don't draw attention to ourselves. What are you trying to do?"

Nicholas shook his head. "Something very weird is going on here." He turned toward Ethan, his eyes troubled. "If we weren't this far back in time, I could swear I just got zapped with some kind of invisible electric security shield."

His expression was so serious that Ethan didn't know how to respond. Nicholas went on. "If those puppets aren't alive, then someone went to a lot of special trouble to cast a spell to keep anyone in this crowd from touching them."

The show ended. A miniature gilded curtain came down, only to rise again as the puppets bowed to the audience's applause. Ethan applauded too, while Nicholas just watched, nursing his wounded hand. A red welt was forming on the side of his palm, as if he'd been burned.

The applause had barely died down when a long black drape screening the platform from the fairway parted. A slim, lithe figure

61

bounded out.

"Don't go, my friends, don't go yet. Not before you have seen the sideshow. The intermission frolic. The game of Pyrth the Puppeteer." The puppeteer stepped farther into the light, pushing right past Nicholas and Ethan, and deposited a curiously wrought trunk on the ground in front of the stage.

Pyrth doffed his peaked and belled cap, and bowed low. The people cheered, and he bounced up to face them. The puppeteer couldn't have been much more than twenty. His hair, a tumble of longish brown curls, framed a round, boyish face that was both mischievous and innocent. Ethan liked him at once.

Pyrth scanned the crowd, his sparkling hazel eyes shifting color, from gold, to green, to brown. His gaze rested on Nicholas and Ethan a moment, then quickly moved on.

"We were supposed to stick together." Olwyn's voice startled Nicholas.

"Sorry," he apologized, and started to tell her about the puppet show. "I've never seen anything like it. It's as if — "

"Shhhhhhh!" Olwyn silenced him. "What's going on now?"

The puppet master had drawn back his flowing sleeves and unlocked the chest. He faced his audience and put a silencing finger to his lips. "My lovelies dance best when it is quiet."

"His what?" Ethan asked.

"Quiet, boy!" several voices warned.

Pyrth's eyes turned in their direction. He arched his fine brows and made a clownish face.

"You are not from Cynwyd," he said, and danced a little toward them. Olwyn tugged on the boys' sleeves, drawing them back a little into the shadows. "So you probably have not heard of my shop and my show," the puppeteer went on. "The show you can see now — my trained and oh-so-special lizards. But come into the town tomorrow and I will show you more of what my puppets can do, boy."

Pyrth danced and twirled and took a piece of glowing yellow chalk out of his pocket. He bent down and drew a large circle in the sand. Then he reached into the ebony chest and produced first one lizard, then another, and another, until there were at least twenty of them. They stood only seven or eight inches high, and each was as different from the others as flowers in a spring meadow. Some had scales that glittered silver or blue or vivid green. Others had hides more like the smooth patterned skin of snakes. Some had crested heads and spiked growths down their spines. All shimmered in the torchlight with a fierce sort of beauty. Nicholas thought it strange that all their eyes were hooded by thick lids. Yet the lizards paraded around the circle never stepping out of its boundary, not seeming the least bit blind.

"My lovelies will now perform for you — would you like to see them dance?" Pyrth asked the crowd. A chorus of "ayes" went up. Pyrth clapped his hands, and the lizards fell back in a long line. "Sparkler, Tingler, Smokey," he shouted, and three lizards stepped out of the line. They stood up on their hind legs and joined their front claws together, as if they were holding hands. The puppeteer pulled a pipe from his pocket and began to blow a merry, drunken sort of tune. The lizards leapt round and round the circle, comically kicking their legs.

Ethan frowned as he watched them. The dance was funny but very peculiar. "He's making fun of them," he said, turning toward Olwyn.

He would have said more, but the expression on Olwyn's face stopped him. Her hands were pressed to her temples and her eyes were closed tight. She seemed to be listening for something. Ethan watched her, puzzled, until the puppeteer said, "But my lovelies can do more than just dance. They are highly trained performers, unlike their fairy tale relatives, the dragons."

A snicker rippled through the crowd.

Nicholas shook his head slowly. "Fairy tale creatures?" he repeated, amazed that anyone on this side of time didn't believe in dragons.

"Look how obedient," Pyrth went on. He clapped his hands again. "See how they come to their names: Finney, tread that wheel." One of the smaller lizards — a sad purplish creature — stumbled out of the chorus line and approached a small wooden wheel. Like a gerbil inside a cage, he mounted the wheel and performed amazing tricks standing on his front legs or balancing on his long, spiked tail. With every trick the crowd laughed louder.

"This is making me sick," Nicholas muttered. "He's got them trained like little slaves."

"I know," Ethan agreed. "It feels all wrong. No one should capture or train them. They look too much like — like baby dragons!" The roar of the crowd had died down for a moment and Ethan's last words rang out loud and clear.

The puppeteer's head snapped around in Ethan's direction. "Boy, did you say dragons?"

Ethan shrank back. Pyrth faced his audience and flashed them a conspiratorial smile. Then he turned back to Ethan. "So what can you tell me about dragons?"

Ethan met his eyes directly. "Well, sir, I've met a few dragons — three to be exact, and — "

Someone jeered, then a tall bone of a man near Ethan spoke up. "He's just a child. He's entitled to believe these stories." He bent down and patted Ethan on the head.

"But they aren't stories," Nicholas insisted.

The puppeteer raised an eyebrow. "You have seen these four, or was it forty, dragons too?" Before Nicholas could respond, Pyrth clapped his hands, and two more "lizards" joined the purple-scaled Finney in a tumbling act.

"If those are lizards, then I am a dragon," Olwyn muttered, pushing her way between the two brothers.

"What are you doing?" Ethan asked.

"Getting a closer look." Olwyn stepped purposefully into the circle. The lizards stopped tumbling. The purple one staggered toward her, and for a moment Ethan caught the brilliant flicker of light as the lids shot up over its whirling eyes: one was blue, one was purple. As Olwyn reached out her hand to touch the tiny beast Pyrth suddenly danced his way up to her.

"Olwyn, watch out!" Nicholas warned, and started toward the circle.

66

The puppeteer snapped his fingers.

"Don't you hurt her!" Ethan yelled — then blinked as Olwyn vanished.

Nicholas rubbed his eyes. "Olwyn?" The word formed on his lips but no sound came out. A moment later he had completely forgotten that a girl named Olwyn had ever existed.

Nicholas turned around and crossed back out of the circle, wondering what he had been doing there anyway. He hunkered down on the ground next to his brother. "Some show, isn't it," he said, his eyes sparkling with delight.

"The best. Back home he could sell this act to a circus," Ethan agreed. "Pyrth's Leaping Lizards."

Eight

Dragon Tales

The puppeteer's show ended just as night fell. Ethan let himself be carried along with the crowd that was heading down the main fairway, past the busy stalls and booths. He wrapped his arms around himself. The nights were cold here, as cold as home, though Cynwyd lay in what seemed to be the middle of a desert. He wished he had worn his down vest beneath the loose wool overshirt. And he wished, as he reached behind his glasses to rub his eyes, that his eyes weren't so scratchy.

But though he was cold and uncomfortable, Ethan still felt as if he was having the best time of his life. "Isn't this great?" he said, turning around expecting to find Nicholas right behind him. There was a trio of men who were, like him, laughing and rubbing their eyes. *Must be something in the air,* Ethan thought.

"Sure," the tall, bony man responded with a

69

wink. "Must be dragons."

Ethan's eyes widened and then he laughed. "Yeah — that's a good one. Dragons!"

"See," a second man said, elbowing the first one, "He was teasing the puppeteer — all of us." He turned to Ethan and pounded his shoulder hard, practically knocking him over. "I bet you're an apprentice to that storytelling lot down by the east gate. Telling Pyrth you've met up with not one, or two, but three dragons . . . "

"Me — a storyteller?" Ethan asked. For some reason the idea struck him as very funny. "No, I'm just from Boston."

"Northern Reaches?" asked the first man, scratching his scruffy beard. "Never heard of it."

Still laughing, Ethan waved and let the men pass by, then turned around to find his brother.

Nicholas had lagged behind, dragging his feet. He was strangely reluctant to leave the stage area. He kept searching the ground as if he had lost something. Just a short while ago the puppeteer had shouldered his trunk, stuffed a couple of the smaller lizards into his pocket, and wandered off whistling into the night. Before he disappeared through the gate leading into town, he had turned around and reminded Nicholas that a visit to his shop the next day might be very rewarding.

"Nicholas, what in the world are you doing here?" Ethan had retraced his steps to the puppet theater, only to find his brother staring distractedly at the partially rubbed out chalk circle on the ground. Nicholas looked up and grinned. "Uh — I don't know." His voice was blurred and slow, and he, too, was rubbing his eyes.

"Come on, let's get going. I heard there's a group of storytellers camped by the town's east gate. Maybe they've got a bonfire, and I'm getting awfully cold."

Nicholas felt too restless for stories, but the prospect of warming his hands at a fire was too good to resist. Besides, it was clear that whatever it was he might have lost wasn't going to be found. So, with a careless shrug, he followed Ethan to the east gate.

The circle of listeners turned out to be friendly, and made room for the boys. A girl with long, dark hair and sparkling black eyes ladled stew into deep pewter bowls then brought them to the brothers. She smiled a particularly friendly smile at Nicholas. He smiled back, a little confused. The girl reminded him of someone. No, not someone so much as some*thing*. He thanked her for the food, and dug into his pocket, producing two silver coins.

"At the tent of the storyteller, food is free for the asking," the girl told him.

Nicholas thanked her again, then stared at the money in his hand. "Where did this come from?"

"Quiet, Nicholas, I'm listening. This is a really great story." Ethan dunked a slab of bread into his stew and took a bite.

Nicholas sighed. The story of dragons and a mythic time back in the childhood of mankind was pretty but boring. As soon as he finished his supper, he returned his plate. Then he slipped out of the firelight and wandered eastward across the fairgrounds and out into the cold night. As he walked he whistled the tune piped by the puppeteer, remembering the "Leaping Lizards," as Ethan had called them.

After a while the hillside sloped up more steeply, and the ground grew rockier underfoot. Nicholas looked up to see where he was going. Directly in front of him, silhouetted in the light of the rising moon, was a huge spreading oak and beyond it, a jagged rock.

The sensation that he had lost something back at the fairground suddenly grew stronger. Nicholas reached up to see if he could touch the oak's lowest branch, and as he did he felt a strange squirming in his pocket. "What the — " he started to exclaim, then something kicked him hard in the stomach, and he went reeling backward onto the ground.

Nicholas landed hard with a thump. But that was nothing compared to the shock he got when something huge and fiery suddenly burst from his pocket and swirled with a joyous roar up into the sky. Nicholas rubbed his eyes; the sandy feeling had vanished.

"Fingal?" he gasped. "Is that really you?"

Moonlight danced in rainbows off the dragon's familiar glittering purple scales. The huge eyes whirled with joy, the right eye purple, the left one blue.

"Nicholas Lord!" Fingal threw his mighty head back and belched a wreath of phosphorescent steam. "Am I glad it's *you!*"

"Where did you come from? What are you doing here?"

"Out of your pocket is where I have come from. And as to what I am doing here — " Fingal's eyes grew dark as coal pits. "I was enspelled. I was shrunk down into what you humans call — a — a — lizard." He spat the last word out and his hide twitched violently, making his scales jangle.

Nicholas's head suddenly felt as if it were going to burst. He clutched his temples, then as quickly as it started the awful feeling was gone. For the first time since watching Pyrth's show, his head was clear, and all at

once he began to remember.

"It's the puppeteer," Nicholas said. "He's behind whatever's going on. Oh, Fingal — I'm so sorry I laughed at you."

"You could not help that," Fingal said, rather sadly. "For you were enspelled too — as soon as Pyrth transformed Olwyn — "

"Olwyn! That's what's been lost!" Nicholas looked at the dragon helplessly. "Where is she? What has he done to her?"

Fingal looked down. His eyes had turned a troubled pale blue. "I feel terrible. She tried to touch me. If she had, she would have known for sure who I am, who all the lizards are. The puppeteer could not stand for that, so he did to her what he does to all his enemies. He made her disappear. She must be somewhere inside his circle of power." The dragon sighed a fiery sigh. "I don't know exactly what happened to her, or to all the others he has hated over the years. The other lizards say that they just vanished."

Nicholas sat down beneath the tree. "Pyrth must be very powerful if he can enspell dragons."

"Oh, well," Fingal said, settling down and starting to groom the scales on his legs. "That power isn't really his. It came from Breton."

"The sorcerer — but I thought he was dead."

"Oh, he is," Fingal said rather breezily, then shifted his position so he was eye to eye with Nicholas. "But years ago with Breton's help, the puppeteer invoked a magic circle."

"Olwyn felt it when she passed this tree today," Nicholas said.

Fingal nodded. "She would, of course. The oak marks the border. Any dragon who crosses the boundary shrinks to a lizard and ends up in Pyrth's show."

Nicholas grunted. "After the little time I spent with Breton, I wouldn't say he was the sort of guy to do anyone any favors."

Fingal laughed darkly. "Ah, but sorcerers must have their allies too. When Breton stole Angarth's pearl, he sought shelter with Pyrth, who back then was just an ordinary sort of man — with great skill at puppet making and a ripe streak of dishonesty. As a kind of thank-you present for harboring him, Breton gave Pyrth a cycle of spells. One of them kept away the dragons who protect this portion of the Seven Kingdoms from dark magic. Another created the magic circle. Unless an enspelled dragon can find his way back across the boundary of the circle, he is trapped in his lizard form forever."

"But you did it, just now."

Fingal bristled with pride. "Yessss, I did," he said with a definite hiss of pleasure. Then

76

he cast an affectionate eye on Nicholas. "But not without *your* help — and as far as I know I am the only dragon that has ever escaped. Pyrth keeps a tight watch on us, and we are quite powerless when we are in lizard form. We retain our intelligence, and our understanding of language, but we cannot speak to humans, nor can we fly."

"That explains the empty space Olwyn felt in this part of the kingdom. It all has to do with the puppeteer and his magic," Nicholas said, trying to piece together the story. "But how *did* you get out? I mean, how in the world did you land in my pocket?"

"You might call it luck — I believe that is the human term, though there really is no such thing from a dragon's point of view. The universe dances to a complicated but very well planned pattern. You did not come to Cynwyd by accident. I probably could not have escaped with any other human but you or Ethan, for though the Puppeteer cast his spell on you, there was a moment when you almost saw Olwyn vanish. That moment was a gap between his magic and its effect on you, and that's when I hopped into your pocket." The dragon hesitated, looking slightly puzzled. "I think it was possible because you are from a different time, but we will have to ask an older, wiser dragon about that. All I know is that you were meant to be here."

Nicholas nodded slowly. "That's probably right. Olwyn called us back to Nir, but we landed here. She thought she wasn't strong enough to make her own magic work."

"Olwyn didn't call you here. I think something bigger did. It is important that the dragons be freed now, though truthfully, I do not see why this time was chosen. There must be trouble brewing in the land."

"Well, Angarth is missing — " Nicholas said, then reeled a little beneath Fingal's startled roar.

"Wait, Fingal. Don't panic," Nicholas corrected himself. "I don't know if Angarth is missing, but Griffen is. Olwyn was searching for him. He was last seen with Angarth, but for two months' time there's been no news of either of them."

"That is still troubling news, which makes it all the more urgent," said the dragon. "You must help me free the other dragons tonight. If Angarth is in danger, we all must be able to come to his aid."

This is getting complicated, thought Nicholas. *Now we have to find people for Drazyl, find Griffen for Olwyn, and free the other dragons — all by full moon.* But all he said to Fingal was, "If you cross the line, you get small again, don't you?"

78

Fingal nodded gravely. "Yes. I don't like it, but I trust you. I can hide in your pocket. We'll go to the puppetmaker's shop, and release the other dragons. We'll need Ethan's help though. You can't carry all of us off on your own."

"That's easier said than done," Nicholas sighed. "You see, part of the puppetmaker's trickery is to make us not believe in dragons. Ethan doesn't believe you exist anymore."

Fingal looked shocked. "Ethan? He feels this?"

"Only since Olwyn vanished. I felt the same way until I saw you. I just hope I don't forget about this conversation once we go back over the line."

"You won't. I know that Pyrth's blinding spell is short-lived. Ethan will snap out of it when he sees for himself the evil that puppeteer can do." Fingal craned his long neck and tilted his head back toward the stars. "The night grows late. We must hurry back to the town before they close the gates." With that he deliberately spread his wings and flew back over the tree. Nicholas raced to keep up with him. A second later a small purple lizard landed with a thump at his feet.

Nicholas pocketed Fingal and headed for the twinkling lights of the town.

Nine

Fair Game

"You want to do *what*?" Ethan stared in disbelief at his older brother.

Nicholas took a deep breath. "Listen, Brainwave, there's no time to lose explaining it all again. We need to get into Cynwyd before the closing of the gates. We have to find the puppeteer's shop and free the lizards. Trust me," Nicholas pleaded. "This is important."

"Trust you?" Ethan scoffed. "I'm beginning to think you actually *believe* that tale about a dragon who guards a castle beneath the sea. And now you expect me to swallow this crazy story about the lizards really being dragons who were caught in an evil spell." With a sigh, Ethan turned back to the bonfire.

Inside Nicholas's pocket, Fingal kicked his legs hard. Nicholas didn't need words to understand the signal: There was no more time to waste.

"Suit yourself," Nicholas said with a shrug. "You're really going through with this? You're breaking into Pyrth's store to steal the lizards?"

Nicholas didn't answer. He kept walking toward the arched east gate in the town's wall.

To his surprise he heard Ethan hurrying to catch up with him.

Ethan fell in step at his side. "Well, I still think that's a pretty crazy story about dragons, but it gives me the creeps to see animals cooped up like that and trained just to make people laugh. It doesn't seem right."

"So you'll help?" Nicholas looked at his brother.

"Yeah," Ethan said, "but we'd better hurry. That guy at the gate looks like he's about to close it!"

The boys slipped inside the town walls, not a moment too soon. They had barely turned the corner and headed down a crooked, cobblestone street when the gatekeeper blew a warning horn. Three times the mournful sound filled the night, followed by the clang of the huge iron gate slamming shut.

Nicholas turned the corner onto a broad, straight avenue of shuttered shops.

"How do you know where you're going?" Ethan gave his brother a puzzled look. "You haven't been here before, have you?"

"Of course I haven't, Toadbrain." Nicholas clamped his mouth shut and didn't say more. If Ethan temporarily didn't believe in dragons, he certainly wasn't going to believe that one of Pyrth's lizards was in his pocket, directing Nicholas right to the store by little taps and scrapes with his claws.

Up ahead and to the left, a carved wooden sign hung out over the street: PYRTH, SON OF NYMANDS, MASTER PUPPETEER.

"This is the place," Ethan said, more than a little awed. "You sure have a great sense of direction."

Nicholas accepted the compliment, then turned his attention to the problem of getting through the door.

"Try the handle," Ethan suggested.

Nicholas eyed his brother with disgust, but to humor him he tried to lift the latch. The door swung open. "I don't believe this," Nicholas muttered.

"Neither do I," Ethan admitted quickly. "I was being sarcastic."

Nicholas closed the door behind him, not wanting to draw attention from any passerby. By now all the lights on the street were out.

It took a moment for their eyes to adjust to the darkness of the shop. "The shutters," Ethan suggested. "I bet you can open them

82

from inside."

"We don't need to," Nicholas said with a grim laugh. "Look at your arm. We seem to be walking flashlights." The tattoos on their wrists were glowing softly in the dark, lighting all but the farthest corners of the small room.

"The dragons should be over here, in this trunk," Nicholas went on, talking to himself as he grabbed a burlap sack from a pile near the door.

"Everything feels so — so alive in here," Ethan said, not quite admitting how spooked he was. Inside a glasslike case, rows of puppets were displayed. Several were clamped into little wooden stands on top of the counter, their web-thin strings draped neatly around their feet. The puppets' eyes seemed to follow Ethan as he studied them. One he hadn't seen in the show caught his eye. It was a girl puppet, with long blond braids, blue eyes, and the silliest skirt he'd ever seen. She was seated on a stool, next to a lifelike puppet cow, whose eyes were shut and seemed to be sleeping. Ethan had a terrible urge to pull one of her pigtails. His hand reached out. Before he could touch her, Nicholas let out a startled cry.

"Olwyn's lute, and her dress. I swear it!" Nicholas whirled on his heels, holding out a

83

lute and a crimson dress.

"Olwyn?"

"The girl — the girl we met. Griffen's daughter. You remember Griffen." Nicholas put down the lute and dress, and shook the younger boy by the shoulders.

"Of course I remember Griffen, but his — his what?" Ethan suddenly couldn't find the word that was on the tip of his tongue. He blinked then looked down. The instrument at Nicholas's feet glowed in the wyrmlight. Ethan couldn't take his eyes off it. He reeled a little and the memory of Olwyn flooded him like a tide. "Olwyn — " The word came out thick and hard on his tongue. "Olwyn." He swayed a little, and would have fallen if Nicholas hadn't caught him.

"You do remember now," Nicholas said quietly. "I can see that. But why would the puppeteer want us to forget her at the show?"

"Whatever the reason," Ethan said, sounding more like himself, "she's around here somewhere. She wouldn't have wandered off and left her dress. And she'd never leave her lute — "

Ethan bounded back to the counter. "Nicholas, come quick!" Before Nicholas could get there, Ethan took a chance and tweaked the milkmaid's braid.

"Stop that you, you, you brain of a toad!"

The little voice squeaked with anger.

"It *is* alive, and it's Olwyn!" Ethan freed her from the stand, and picked her up. She was about a foot tall, and her voice had changed too. She squirmed to get out of Ethan's grasp.

"Stop it, Olwyn," Nicholas commanded. "We're trying to help you. There are lizards somewhere in here, and I've got to free them. They're really dragons." To prove it, he reached into his pocket and produced Fingal, carefully setting the little dragon on the counter. "This 'Finney' is really Fingal. He can't talk in this form, or fly, or breathe fire, but he can understand us and signal us. Now, there's no time to lose."

"You can say that again," Olwyn fumed. "You can't just walk into a magician's shop and expect him not to notice. Spells of warning encircle this place."

"The lizards are in that trunk," Olwyn said, pointing to the opposite corner.

Quickly, Ethan and Nicholas threw open the trunk to the hiss of snarling lizards. "Fingal," Nicholas called, nursing a pair of nipped fingers, "tell them we mean them no harm. We're going to free them — *all of them*." But the enspelled dragons didn't need to hear more. They quieted down and allowed the boys to bundle them into the burlap sack.

86

"Hurry," Olwyn cried from the counter. "I hear footsteps. Pyrth's coming. There's a way out the back, behind the curtain."

"Get Olwyn and Fingal," Nicholas ordered his brother.

Ethan grabbed Olwyn around the waist and stuffed Fingal into the sack. Nicholas shouldered the heavy sack and shoved Ethan out in front of him just as the front door burst open.

"Stop, thieves! Stop, I say!" Pyrth exploded, as the boys dashed out into the back alley.

Ten

Hunted

"Oh, if I could only help!" Olwyn cried. Ethan could barely hear her over the pounding of his feet against the pavement. "I'm making everything worse. You have to carry me and Nicholas has all the dragons."

"Don't worry," Ethan shouted back, "you'll get your chance." *If*, he thought to himself, Nicholas was right. "Once we're out of the circle of power you'll be normal-sized again, and you can help us figure out what to do."

"And don't forget the dragons," Olwyn's shout sounded like a whisper. "They'll be bigger too, and they'll regain their powers."

"Take a left here," Nicholas shouted from up ahead, suddenly changing course. "I think the west gate is still open. People are coming from that direction and I haven't heard the warning horn blow again." He swerved to the left, rounded the corner, and pelted down a winding cobblestone street. Ethan followed and they emerged back onto the main avenue that housed all the shops.

From several blocks away, Pyrth finally caught sight of them and his voice rang through the night, "Stop, thieves! Stop them! They've stolen my lizards!"

"He's going to have the whole town after us," Ethan gasped, wondering how much longer he could keep up this pace.

"Just keep going." Nicholas fell back behind Ethan. "Don't look back, no matter what happens. Keep going and get Olwyn out of here. Remember the tree. If we get separated, go straight for the oak tree."

Ethan nodded breathlessly. But hope lay just ahead. The keeper of Cynwyd's west gate hadn't heard Pyrth's outcry. A knot of traders was loitering just outside the town wall, watching a flame-juggling acrobat perform. The gatekeeper was watching too, his back to the town.

The sight made Ethan forget the cramps in his legs. With a final burst of speed, he plunged through the gate and into the crowded fairway.

The gatekeeper leaped to attention. "STOP!" he yelled, and began pulling on the stout rope that rang the town's alarm bell.

Nicholas doubled his already fast pace and aimed himself directly at the gatekeeper.

Behind him Pyrth shouted, "Stop that boy!"

The gatekeeper never even saw Nicholas. He let go of the bell pull and grabbed his club. Then he and several of the traders started after Ethan. Nicholas neatly sideswiped the gatekeeper, sending the heavy man sprawling flat on his face.

Nicholas forced himself to keep running. The heavy sack full of lizards banged against his back with every step as he raced after Ethan, beyond the fairground and onto the moonlit plain. But though the crowd dropped back, Pyrth was gaining on him, and Nicholas knew he didn't have the strength to outlast the puppeteer.

"Give up now," Pyrth shouted. To Nicholas's dismay the puppeteer didn't even sound winded. "I'll be easy on you, boy. Just slow down and we'll talk."

The voice was growing dangerously close. Nicholas gritted his teeth. *Never*, he thought. Fury at what the puppeteer had done to the dragons and Olwyn fueled him. He fought to make his legs keep going, then he took heart. The ground was already sloping upward to the crest of the hill. Nicholas aimed himself at the moonlit outline of the mighty oak.

Just when the ground beneath his feet became broken and stony, the moonlight vanished. An unnatural dark cloud swirled up from the ground, shrouding the world in a black mist. As Fingal had warned him, Pyrth was capable of powerful magic.

Up ahead, Ethan cried out, and a small avalanche of pebbles skittered down the dry slope. Nicholas winced, realizing his brother had tripped in the spell-made darkness. "Keep going, Ethan!" Nicholas shouted. "Get up and keep going. Save Olwyn!"

"I can see," Ethan shouted back . "Look at your arm. The wyrm tattoo — it's glowing again!"

For a moment Nicholas glanced down at his wrist. Ethan was right. The wyrm's whole body throbbed with a pale green light. It wasn't very bright, but it pierced the inky fog just enough to show the way up the hill and toward the tree.

Ethan stumbled past the tree — and out of the fog. Once he passed through Pyrth's circle of power, the nearly full moon shone bright again. Ethan whirled quickly, trying to find Nicholas, who was still caught in the dark.

"Tell him to throw the sack past the tree." Olwyn's tiny whisper made Ethan look down.

"You're still tiny," he said. "The spell, it didn't break!"

"It must be a different spell than the one Pyrth used on the dragons. Don't worry about me now," Olwyn said impatiently. "Put me down, on the rock, and yell as loudly as you can to your brother. Hurry or Pyrth will catch him. Tell him to throw the sack full of lizards toward you. Then duck!"

Ethan didn't stop to think about what he was doing. "Nicholas," he shouted, hoping his voice carried through the magical fog. "The lizards, toss them to me."

Nicholas could barely make out Ethan's voice, or the direction it was coming from. His heart felt as if it would burst. He lost his footing, and almost stumbled. He could feel the puppeteer closing on him.

Nicholas plunged forward but fell short of the old oak. The puppeteer's hands closed on his ankles like a trap.

"Ooooowwwww!" Nicholas cried, hitting the ground hard. The sack flew out of his arms — and landed at Ethan's feet. With a burst of flame and the roar of a hundred dragons tore the sky.

Ethan cried out, shielding his face from the terrible light.

"Help Nicholas!" Olwyn shouted with all her strength.

Ethan forced himself to look up. For a moment he was blinded. The sky was filled with dragons, whirling, spitting fire, raging at the puppeteer whose magic circle kept him safe from them.

Nicholas lay sprawled on his face. His arms and head were safely beyond the circle of power, but the puppeteer had hold of his feet and was pulling him back over the invisible magic line.

Ethan reached out and grabbed his brother's hands. "Hold on tight!" he shouted, and tried with all his might to pull Nicholas free of the puppeteer's grasp. Instead, he himself was pulled forward. Then something strong grabbed his own legs. "Just hold onto Nicholas!" a mighty voice shouted.

Ethan looked back. "Fingal?" he cried with joy. "You're here!"

"Don't go back over the circle," Nicholas gasped.

"No need," Fingal said calmly. Then, with one claw anchored in Ethan's jeans, he yanked both boys clear of the circle.

Nicholas got up, feeling a bit dizzy. The puppeteer sat in a heap at the bottom of the hill, still clutching Nicholas's hightops. "I'll have my revenge for this!" Pyrth screamed. "You've stolen my prize jewels, my life's blood, but you cannot steal my power. Now all of Cynwyd will pay dearly."

A stream of angry words floated back to the boys as the defeated puppeteer picked himself up and made his way back to the town.

Olwyn finally broke the silence. "Well,

we're safe."

"Olwyn?" Nicholas looked around, then down a little. She was standing at his feet. "What happened to you?" he cried, amazed.

"Nothing," she replied sadly. "I don't know why, but my spell didn't break." She looked around her and smiled. "But at least they're all right." She gestured toward the huge winged figures. Some were still gliding in the sky, cutting dragon silhouettes against the moon.

"Only as long as we never cross that circle again," Fingal said quietly.

"But the other puppets must be freed, and we can't do it alone," Olwyn said. "I don't even know how to break the spell that's on me. I'm sure one of you — "

A particularly old and crusty dragon flew up and landed several yards away. Carefully, it draped its long tail down the far side of the hill.

"As Eldest of this gathering of the Winged Many," he said, using the dragons' own name for themselves, "I thank you for saving us. We will never forget you, Ethan and Nicholas Lord, already known as friends of Angarth. Nor you, Olwyn, of whom we have heard much from your father."

"You've seen him?" Olwyn's voice rose with hope.

"I have not. Fingal was the last to see him."

"Back in Nir," Fingal admitted sadly.

Olwyn's face dropped. "Yes, of course. You've been enspelled here. You've had no news yourself then. I had hoped to find him. He's supposed to be here, but I — I — "

"Perhaps among the other puppets?" Fingal suggested. "The puppeteer has many trunks of puppets. He might store a loremaster in a more well-guarded place, knowing his powers are great."

"I thought of that back at the shop, but now — "

Nicholas followed her gaze back over the plain. "Now we go back and get him somehow."

"Get all the puppets," Ethan added quietly. "That Pyrth is a real nasty number. We can't leave here until we set the puppets free. They're all real people, with real lives and families, and he has them trapped."

"But we don't know what will break the spell," Fingal said, and turned toward Lyoth. "You, Eldest, are you not learned in magic?"

Lyoth lowered several pairs of translucent lids over his dark green eyes. His voice smoldered as he said, "Those people are Cynwydians. I will never help them. They laughed at us — some even before the puppeteer trapped them. They showed us no compassion in lizard form. Now we will spare no compassion for them."

"That stinks!" Nicholas said, looking Lyoth right in the eye.

No human had ever contradicted the dragon before, and his eyes whirled open wide. "Pardon?" he said.

"That's rotten," Nicholas said. "It's not those people's fault they were enspelled. For a while, neither of us believed in dragons either. We couldn't help it. That's just part of the puppeteer's basket of tricks. But if you won't help us, I know someone who will."

Fingal shifted his weight from foot to foot, and looked very embarrassed. "Oh dear," he moaned. "I am afraid I cannot help you either, now. I cannot disobey Lyoth. I am a very young dragon and — "

"Don't worry, Fingal, we understand." Ethan reached up to stroke Fingal's scales. "You would help us if you could. But Nicholas wasn't talking about you."

"I do not want to hear this conversation," Lyoth broke in. "I must cast a warning spell around this part of the kingdom so that no dragon can ever stumble across this magic circle again. We leave here tomorrow." With that, the ancient dragon bowed to the boys, and a moment later all the dragons except Fingal wheeled lazily up into the sky, flying a complicated pattern and blowing out smoke and ash.

"They're leaving the mark of danger around this place," Fingal explained. Then he turned to the boys. "I cannot disobey Lyoth, but I will stay a little longer and see if perhaps there is not something I might still be permitted to do."

"I think this is where Drazyl comes in," Ethan said. "That's who we meant before. He isn't bound by Lyoth's ruling — he's never been Pyrth's captive."

"Noooo," Fingal said thoughtfully. "He lives in the castle beneath the sea, in Landesferne."

"You know Drazyl?" Nicholas was surprised.

"Of course. All dragons know each other. We can share our minds when we want to. He is as lonely as I was back in my cave where you found me."

"Right, and he needs people to help," Ethan said. "We promised to bring him some. Drazyl can help the puppets — that'll be perfect."

"Except, Toadbrain," Nicholas reminded Ethan sharply, "that he's a dragon, and he'll be shrunk down to lizard size if he sets foot or wing past that tree."

"I thought of that," Ethan admitted. "But still I think we should find him and see if he can come up with a solution."

"But there's no time to go find this Drazyl!" Olwyn leapt to her feet and stalked impatiently in front of the boys. "That puppeteer is up to no good, and I don't think the puppets will be safe with him. Don't forget — he promised revenge."

"You think we should forget about Drazyl and just go back ourselves?" Nicholas asked.

Olwyn nodded.

"Maybe we can do both," Ethan said after a moment's thought. "Nicholas," he pointed at his brother's bare feet, "you've lost your shoes. You're no good for walking anyway." Turning to Fingal Ethan continued, "And you want to help us without breaking Lyoth's rules. He didn't say you couldn't bring Nicholas back to the Guarded Sea. It would take you maybe a couple of hours. If we tried it on foot it would take over a day."

Fingal reached up with a talon and scratched his head. "Wouldn't I still be helping Cynwyd? Lyoth forbade that."

"Yes and no," Ethan said slowly. "You see, Nicholas and I are on a quest. Drazyl made us promise to bring him people to guard and protect before the next full moon. If we don't, we'll become his prisoners beneath the sea."

Fingal began to shimmer from the top of his horned head to the tip of his tail. "I can do this then — Lyoth would not forbid my helping you. Climb onto my back, and we should reach the sea just after the dawn."

Olwyn warmed to Ethan's plan. "And meanwhile, Ethan and I can creep down to the town. We can lose ourselves in the fair crowd and keep an eye on the puppets at least. Perhaps we'll find a way to free them ourselves once we're there."

Ethan and Olwyn waited until Nicholas took off on Fingal's back, then they headed back down to Cynwyd. They stuck to the shadows of the plain, moving as silently as cats.

The night was late and the moon had almost set when they reached the edge of the town. There was no way through the locked gates, so they found shelter in a dry snowberry thicket that grew against the wall. Exhausted from the day's adventures, Olwyn curled up in the warmth of Ethan's palm, and together they drifted off into a dark, deep, and dreamless sleep.

Eleven

A Sea Change

It seemed only a moment later when Ethan opened his eyes to a gray dawn sky. Through a cold mist the sun shone pale over the rim of the eastern mountains. In spite of the chill in the air, Ethan felt strangely content. Comfortable even. A pleasant jangling tune he couldn't quite place was running through his head.

"Where am I?" he asked, sitting up and rubbing his eyes.

"In the middle of a snowberry thicket, outside the town gates." Olwyn sounded as if she was in a remarkably good mood for a person about to set out on a dangerous mission. She sat on a flat rock not far from Ethan's feet, her small body swaying as she sang a squeaky tune.

"To the sea I will go Be there rain, be there snow Where the dark weeds grow And the sea wyrms dance below."

Olwyn finished the song and smiled at Ethan. "We have to free the puppets," she said.

Ethan smiled back. He put the doll-sized Olwyn on his shoulder and tried to walk toward the east gate, the one leading to the puppeteer's street. Instead, his feet forced him toward the main west gate.

Traders and performers straggled out of tents, still in their nightshirts, their eyes sleepy but their faces smiling. "To the sea we will go Be there rain, be there snow . . . " All the people were singing versions of Olwyn's song.

Ethan and Olwyn watched as the town gate swung open. A chorus of laughter poured out into the morning, and, in spite of the heavy mist, the sun seemed to shine more brightly.

Dancing backward through the gate came the puppeteer. He was dressed in a striped blue and red jerkin. Silver bells danced on the peak of his hat and the pointed hem of his shirt. He strummed a beautifully inlaid lute as he danced backward down the fairway. As he caught sight of Ethan and the tiny puppet-sized Olwyn, his smile stretched wider across his rosy cheeks. "Join the fun, my little ones," he mocked in a lilting voice. "To the sea with me, where the waves will set you free."

"He's going to drown all the people of Cyn-

101

wyd," Ethan said, realizing what was happening. But there was nothing he could do. Angry as he was, he began to laugh and his feet danced a merry jig to the puppeteer's tune. "We're enspelled, like the dragons were," he cried.

"He's playing my lute!" Olwyn exclaimed. "He's stolen my music." But though her voice trembled and tears danced from the corners of her eyes, her lips were turned up in a bright unnatural smile.

Streaming through the gates after the puppeteer were the puppets. This time, all the sadness was washed from their faces. They sent up light bell-like peals of laughter and danced as if they'd never tire. Behind them came the townspeople of Cynwyd, and behind them the dogs and cats, cows, horses, pigs, and even a few pet turtles. Over the plain they went singing the same refrain, "To the sea we will go Be there rain, be there snow . . . "

At the end of the procession, Olwyn and Ethan fell in with the other traders. "To the sea, to the sea," they sang with the others. Helplessly, they followed the puppeteer, a bright small figure at the head of the merry throng. They followed him up the hill and beyond the tree. They passed through the magic circle, but Pyrth's spell didn't break.

Ethan looked at the old oak longingly. Its

trunk was scorched from the dragonfire the night before, and surrounded by scales — purple, green, silver and blue. He remembered everything that had happened to him and wanted to cry. But all he could do was sing and laugh and follow the puppeteer up and down the hills leading back to the Guarded Sea.

Meanwhile, Nicholas had problems of his own. As promised, Fingal had brought him back to the black grotto. Olwyn's boat still lay safe, high above the waterline. But though Nicholas had climbed to the top of the grotto at the crack of dawn and shouted down at the water at least three times, Drazyl refused to appear.

"Maybe he is asleep," Fingal suggested, pacing the shore and craning his long neck over the waves. "Or hunting?"

"It's no use," Nicholas said, giving up. "He just won't come. I never should have trusted him."

"Let me try," Fingal said. The purple dragon rose up on his hind legs and shot a plume of bright green fire into the sky. A moment later he closed his eyes, opened his mouth very wide, and let out a high-pitched eerie sound.

Nicholas clapped his hands over his ears.

"What was that?"

"Dragoncall. Any dragon within a hundred leagues of here must come."

"Who beckons at my shore?" The watery voice boomed from just below their feet. The waves churned, and an enormous breaker surged over the top of the cliff where Nicholas stood.

Fingal fluttered his massive wings and hovered a few feet over the ground. "I hate getting wet," he grumbled, and cast a dirty look in the direction of the water. A second later, the young dragon's expression changed. "Oooooh, am I going to get in trouble!"

The words were barely out of his mouth when, grumbling and blowing out great clouds of steam, Drazyl rose up out of the waves. Nicholas stumbled back slightly. Seeing Drazyl face to face above water was even more terrifying than it had been down below. The monster seemed twice his underwater size, five times more powerful than Nicholas had ever imagined — and at the moment he was obviously very angry.

"What have you brought me?" Drazyl looked Fingal up and down and made a huge sound of disgust. "A dragon, when what I need is people! For this" — he splashed noisily out of the water, and the ground shook as he set foot on shore — "I break more than promises."

"You cannot harm him," Fingal spoke up bravely, though his voice sounded a little thin. "He is under my — uh — my protection."

Nicholas shook his head. "No, Fingal. I can deal with this. You've helped enough." He glanced up at the sky behind Drazyl's head. Great circles of dragons wheeled in from the east. "I think we've got company. You'd better see to them while I talk to Drazyl."

Fingal hesitated but Nicholas encouraged him to fly off to explain why he had used the dragoncall when he really wasn't in trouble. "I hope he's not in danger," Nicholas murmured, then turned to face the great sea dragon. "Now, Drazyl," he said carefully, "you are wrong. I did not bring you a dragon. The dragon brought me here."

Drazyl studied Nicholas and settled down on his haunches. "Go on," he commanded, and waved a wet, weedy claw in Nicholas's face.

Nicholas wiped off the goop from his cheeks and forced back an angry response. "I've found a whole town full of people who need your help. Now."

The anger in Drazyl's eyes dimmed. "A town? That needs me?" His eyes began to glow, and a rumblelike purr issued from his huge throat. "But I cannot come to a town." He sank back onto the sand and looked very sad. "I cannot leave my hoard."

"No, you can't. Even if you didn't have a hoard. The town is ensnared in a dragonproof spell. But I thought there'd be some other way to help the people." Nicholas quickly outlined the story for Drazyl.

"But what can I do?" asked the dragon as Nicholas ended his tale. "To think there are people in need of me, and I can't go to help them." He got up heavily, and sea water oozed out from between his scales. "Now it is the day of the full moon and," the sea beast heaved a miserable sigh, "I guess I must settle for you and your brother."

"You mean you — you're giving up?" Nicholas stammered, suddenly aware of exactly what Drazyl's decision meant for his own future. "You're just going let those poor people be enspelled by that evil puppeteer and keep us as your prisoners? Are you a dragon or a wyrm?" he asked with great scorn.

Drazyl's nostrils flared dangerously. "Did you *dare* call me a RUMBATHRADRMA-WYRMATHRINGDOATH?" he roared.

Before Nicholas could stammer any sort of reply, Fingal circled in from the east, emitting a series of excited squawks. "They're coming," he called. "All the people of Cynwd are coming. They're led by someone playing a lute."

"People are coming? Here? To me?" Drazyl stretched his wings, which, because they were more finlike than most dragon wings, made it difficult for him to lift himself off the ground. Still, he circled above until he saw what Fingal had described. "Tiny puppets, dancing without strings," he cried. Then he quickly settled back onto the sand. "What you've said is true," he said. "A terrible magician is leading them. I can read his magic: He will drown the puppets and all the living creatures of Cynwyd in the sea."

Fingal hissed, and grabbed Nicholas with his talons and set him firmly on a ledge inside the grotto. "Stay here," he commanded. "I can't help you now. I am forbidden, and my elders are watching from high above. But Drazyl will be true to his word — he has found people to protect."

"But he can hardly fly," Nicholas whispered, positioning himself so he could see out of the cave.

"Don't let that fool you," Fingal assured Nicholas. "Drazyl is almost as mighty as Angarth and definitely as large. Sea dragons have other powers." With that Fingal took to the sky, just as the first few villagers skipped blithely past the puppeteer and into the cold, deadly waves.

"Do something," Nicholas shouted at Drazyl.

Calmly, Drazyl extended a long front leg,

107

and instead of sinking beneath the water, the puppets leading the parade of townspeople danced along his thigh. "I need your help," he bellowed at Nicholas. "If I leave the water, the people will fall off me and drown. You must steal the instrument from the puppeteer."

"Right," Nicholas said, trying to ignore a shiver of fear. "No problem."

Carefully, he edged himself out of the grotto and back up onto the huge black rock. *I couldn't have planned this better,* he realized as he saw that the puppeteer was standing right below him. The sight of his favorite hightops dangling from Pyrth's belt suddenly made him very mad. Nicholas took aim, then jumped down, knocking Pyrth to the ground. The lute flew out of the puppeteer's hands and landed safely in the sand, just out of reach.

The second the music stopped, the procession ground to a halt. People rubbed their eyes as if waking from a dream. Those who had entered the water began wading ashore.

Nicholas dove for the lute at the moment the crowd noticed the dragon flying heavily overhead. "A dragon! A dragon!" the cry went up, and the townspeople screamed in terror.

Amazed, the puppeteer and the townspeople could only stare at the old sea serpent above them. Pyrth recovered first, letting out a merry laugh. "You don't exist, Drazyl," he said, then broke into a language Nicholas couldn't understand: "Drazyl frindyr grimry tyr. Lydo borymyr . . . "

Before Pyrth could complete his spell, Drazyl reared up and shot a narrow laser-thin jet of water at the puppetmaker. A horrible shriek filled the air. And where the puppetmaker had stood, there was now only a small, very wet puppet wearing a red-and-blue striped jerkin.

"You are finished, Pyrth. Your fate will be to live as a toy the rest of your life," Drazyl pronounced in a booming voice. He circled the crowd, then headed back toward the grotto. Slowly he eased himself down, folded his wings around him, and sat proudly surveying the new people of his kingdom.

For a long moment Nicholas stood spellbound, then he grabbed the puppeteer. "You may be small," he told Pyrth, "but I still don't trust you." Carefully, he carried the puppeteer to Olwyn's boat where he bound his wrists, then turned the boat upside down over him. "That should keep you safe for a while. Let the people of Cynwyd decide what to do with you." He brushed off his hands and headed back down the beach.

Ethan was never sure exactly what happened. One minute he was dancing helplessly

109

toward the sea. The next minute the music stopped. He had put Olwyn down and was trying to rub away the ringing in his ears. Then he spotted Drazyl above his head blowing a jet of water toward the earth, *hot* water. "Did you see that?" he said to Olwyn.

Suddenly the puppets were no longer puppets. Pyrth's last spell was broken. Full-sized people appeared on the beach — as if out of the air. Even Ethan, who had been standing there talking to the puppet Olwyn, didn't catch the exact moment of her change. Halfway through a sentence, he was looking down at her; the next moment he was looking up at her.

"You're back to normal!"

"Thanks to you and Nicholas," Olwyn said, grinning. Then her smile faded. "I ought be searching the crowd. My father may be here after all, though — " She paused and her forehead creased in a frown. "Though if he were, I would sense him."

"Maybe when he was under Pyrth's spell, he lost his own powers. Maybe that's why you couldn't sense him." Ethan tried to sound hopeful. But with his white hair, short build, and piercing eyes, Griffen was a distinctive-looking person. He'd stand out anywhere. Ethan looked around.

"I'm going to question some of the others,"

Olwyn told Ethan, and set out into the thick of the crowd.

Ethan's attention was drawn in the opposite direction. A large, somewhat fearful, cluster of villagers was gathered at the base of the black grotto rock. Coiled in splendor at the top was Drazyl. His silvery scales glistened in the morning light, and his head was bent toward a short, round man wearing scarlet hose and a bright yellow jerkin. Ethan recognized him as the tailor from yesterday's puppet show.

"Oh — uh — ummm — ye mighty sea serpent," the tailor stammered, then turned around to the crowd, his whole face begging for someone else to step forward and take this job.

"Yesssss," Drazyl replied graciously, "you were saying — "

The tailor gulped, then someone pushed him forward from behind and he stumbled against the rock. Gently, Drazyl extended a claw and set him back on his feet. The tailor cocked his head, seeming to marvel at the daintiness of the dragon's touch. Taking courage, he went on with his message. "Now that we know dragons exist. . ." he began.

"Dragons exist?" Drazyl repeated, stunned. "Who said we didn't?"

"Pyrth," the villagers cried in unison.

Drazyl looked at the citizens of Cynwyd and

112

pity shone in his golden eyes.

"But we — we would like to ask you if you would come back to Cynwyd with us and become our town dragon."

Drazyl's face fell. "I can't," he said in what was, for him, a very quiet voice.

Ethan spoke up from the back of the crowd. "He can't cross the circle of power. Its magic is far older and more powerful than any magic Pyrth possessed by himself. Breaking Pyrth's hold on the people did not break the dragon-spell."

"If Drazyl crosses the line into Cynwyd, he'll shrink to a lizard and lose his powers," Nicholas said.

Drazyl cleared his throat. "Besides, I would never leave my hoard." He looked at Nicholas and his eyes glinted craftily for a moment. "So we have a problem here. You and your brother must convince these people to live beneath the sea with me. Or you will remain with me forever."

Nicholas faced the crowd and caught his breath. He looked, really *looked* at the people.

"I can't do it," he said, softly, then turned to Drazyl and declared in a loud, clear voice, "I can't send these people into the sea with you. What was the point of saving them from the puppetmaker if they're only going to become

113

your prisoners? No way, Drazyl," he finished, and steeled himself to face Ethan. He had just condemned himself and his brother to spending the rest of their lives at the bottom of the Guarded Sea.

As Nicholas spoke, Ethan paled slightly. But he didn't flinch when Nicholas met his gaze. Ethan squared his shoulders and said, "I feel the same way, too."

"I am not like the puppeteer," Drazyl snarled. "They will live, you know. They will have happy lives. I will even," he added with great difficulty, "share my hoard with them and help them repair the castle and dwellings of Lindesfarne."

Then Olwyn's voice rang out as she pushed her way to the front of the crowd, "Or the people of Cynwyd could move closer to the sea. That way you could stay with your hoard, oh mighty guardian of the Seventy Seas and Forty-four Lakes, *and* protect the people at the same time."

"Build a new city?" the tailor exclaimed, looking rather daunted.

"Why not?" suggested a tall, blond woman, who was dressed as a princess from her days as a puppet, but who was really the head of the carpenters' guild.

"Cynwyd may be safe enough now," she pointed out, "but as soon as the next evil per-

114

son comes around and discovers we lack protection from the dragons, we'll be enspelled once again."

Olwyn nodded. "This woman speaks wisely," she said.

The tailor started to climb up onto Drazyl's rock. "Begging your permission, sir," he said with a stiff, formal bow. Then he turned to face the villagers. "I think we have no choice. Working together to make a new town will help make new lives."

"He speaks the truth," someone said, and the rest of the crowd agreed.

Drazyl cleared his throat and everyone stopped to listen.

"As Guardian of Cynwyd, I will see that the earth between here and the circle of power grows rich and fertile again," he vowed solemnly.

The crowd cheered and Olwyn began to play a merry dance, and this time everyone danced because they were happy.

115

Twelve

Fair Trade

The beach was empty, except for a group of children standing a few feet from Drazyl and watching the giant sea dragon in awe. The rest of the dragons were flying north in formation — perfect X, except for one purpley dragon, that lingered at the fringe. It was Fingal, who had been ordered to join his elders, but hated leaving his Cape Breton friends.

Nicholas surveyed the scene from his perch on the rock. "We're going home," he said, as if he still didn't quite believe it.

Ethan simply smiled. *Home.* At this very moment, at the brink of the Guarded Ocean, he was quite sure he had never heard a more beautiful word in his life.

A stifled sob made him look up. It was Olwyn. In the middle of all the shouting and planning, she had wandered off. Now she was back at the base of the cliff, crying.

"Olwyn?" Ethan shifted his bundle from his

right arm to his left, not quite sure what to do.

Nicholas stared at her a moment, and then he understood. "Your father — he wasn't with the other enspelled puppets."

Olwyn shook her head.

Nicholas hesitated, then said the words Ethan dreaded to hear: "I'll stay here with you. I'll help you search for your father."

Ethan gulped. "Uh — yeah," he said. "Me too, I guess."

"Oh, no you won't!" a watery voice bellowed.

Drazyl had heaved himself out of the sea and now shook the shimmering water off his knifelike scales. "I have made a promise. You cannot stay here. Or — "

Olwyn interrupted in a flat voice. "Or Drazyl cannot be guardian of Cynwyd. It's a rule of magic, Nicholas." She looked up at him, her blue eyes brimming with tears. "Drazyl must keep the exact promise he made."

"But you must have known this all along," Nicholas exclaimed. "You knew if we found the people for Drazyl, then we couldn't help you find Griffen."

Olwyn gave a short laugh. "Yes. Except you forget that I had heard my father had headed toward Cynwyd."

"But he didn't," Ethan said suddenly. "If he

117

had, he would have been with Angarth, and Angarth would have been enchanted like all the other dragons. He never got to Cynwyd. No one saw him there."

Olwyn sat down heavily and began to loosen her braids. "Don't ask me why, but somehow that makes me feel better. Maybe if my father and Angarth had turned up together, the puppetmaker would have worked even a darker sort of magic on them, especially if he'd recognized Griffen's powers." She sighed, and managed a brave smile. "I have no choice but to go on from here. I can join one of the caravans traveling north."

Ethan remembered his vision a few days earlier, of Griffen being in a place full of cold and ice and wind. "Yes," he whispered, "north might be a good direction to go in."

There was a rumbling, throat-clearing sort of sound and an impatient splash as Drazyl dove back into the water and reappeared. "The future demands you come back with me now."

"Olwyn," Nicholas said, strangely reluctant to leave her. "If we can, we'll come back."

She nodded. "Perhaps this wasn't the time for you to help me. I put out a call to you, but maybe another call came before mine."

"That's what Fingal thought," Ethan reminded his brother.

"Now, get out of here," Olwyn shoved the boys down toward the water. "I hate long goodbyes. I hate crying."

Drazyl didn't give the boys time to hear any more. He flapped his wings, and a breaker towered up behind them. A moment later they were swept out to sea. Drazyl lifted himself under them and paddled his way across the surface of the water.

"I am very pleased to have met you. You are worthy friends of Angarth. You are now also friends of Drazyl. Never forget that."

"But where are we going?" Ethan cried, hanging on to the slimy spikes that jutted out from the beast's neck.

"Your home," Drazyl shouted back at him. "Now hold on tight," he warned, then plunged abruptly down. The water closed over the boys.

"Nicholas!" Ethan yelled. "I'm drowning. I'm — "

"You're not drowning at all." Nicholas sounded his usual older brother disgusted self.

Ethan sniffed the air. It *was* air he was breathing and not water. "Where are we?" he asked.

"Open your eyes," Nicholas suggested sarcastically. "Take a look."

"We're at the lighthouse?" Ethan couldn't

believe it. They were indeed on the narrow pebbled beach at the foot of Smugglers' Lighthouse. Arnie Ducheyne's dinghy was beached beside them, full of water. Ethan pushed up his glasses and looked at his brother. Nicholas was staring glumly out to sea, his arms wrapped tightly around his knees. The jerkin he had worn in Cynwyd was gone, but he wasn't wearing his jacket either. He looked miserable and very cold.

"Your sneakers — they're still missing."

"I never got them back from Pyrth," Nicholas moaned. "Now how in the world am I going to explain that to Mom?"

"Or my missing vest," Ethan cried.

"And my jacket."

"We left all that stuff back there, in Cynwyd."

"In *old* Cynwyd," Nicholas pointed out. "Too bad we can't get a message to Olwyn, just in case we do get back to see her again."

Ethan looked out over Frenchman's Bay. The sun was still high in the sky. "Time doesn't seem to pass at all here, when we're in Nir."

"Or Cynwyd." Nicholas dug his fingers into the sand. "I wonder if we really will be able to go back again."

"When we're needed," Ethan said with certainty. "Something or someone will be sure we find a way through to the Seven Kingdoms."

"There you are!" The crusty voice made them jump.

"Drazyl?" Ethan cried, before he turned around. Then his face fell. It was Kevin Mc-Phee, the new lighthouse keeper.

"Your parents are worried sick about you boys." The tall, blond man shoved back his cap and looked from the boys to the water-logged dinghy. "I'd better call them from the house, let them know you're okay."

"But not much time has passed since — " Ethan began.

Nicholas broke in, "Since we borrowed Arnie's boat. Only an hour or so."

"That's enough time to get a mother worried, though she shouldn't," Kevin added in a lower voice. "Can't say I haven't borrowed a boat or two in my day, when I lived across the bay."

"How did they know about the boat?" Ethan asked.

"Arnie found it missing. Was about to report the robbery. Found your jacket all wet and waterlogged and one of your brother's hightops washed up on the shore. Didn't look good. Nope." The lighthouse keeper motioned for the boys to follow him up to the lighthouse. "Put out an alarm. They're organizing a

121

search now. Let's hurry and phone them. Save your parents some fretting," he said as they started up the stone steps twisting around Smugglers' Rock like a narrow switchback road.

The boys looked out to sea. A dark fog was rolling in. They walked through the door in the base of the lighthouse, just as the storm broke.

"I'll get you some hot chocolate after I phone your folks. Hey, did you boys hurt yourselves?" Kevin put a hand on Nicholas's arm and stared in disbelief at the seawyrm. "A tattoo? You're a little young for that, aren't you?"

Nicholas thought quickly. "It's not a real tattoo. These are the kind you wash off." Praying it would work, he went over to the sink, grabbed a sponge, and rubbed at his wrist. Two rubs and the wyrm vanished.

Ethan stretched out his arm, and Nicholas slowly began to wash away the second wyrm, beginning with its tail.

"I kind of hate to see it go," Nicholas murmured as Kevin crossed the room and picked up the wall phone.

"Me too," Ethan sighed. Then, just before Nicholas' sponge touched the creature's slanty green eye, it winked.

"Your folks want to talk to you kids," Kevin

called across the kitchen.

"Here goes nothing," Nicholas groaned.

"Who cares?" Ethan said. "It winked. It really winked!"

And he followed his brother across the tiled floor, studying his arm where he'd worn the sign of Drazyl, the great sea dragon.

It's holiday time for the Lord boys — and they're about to end up with some of the greatest gifts they could ever have imagined. Their only problem is that they may not make it home for the celebration! Griffen, the loremaster, has been taken hostage by an angry dragon who's missing her prize jewel. And if Ethan and Nicholas don't help fast, there will be an all-out dragon war! Don't miss:

DRAGONFIRE #3, The Curse of Peredur